CRANBERRY BLUFF

A Tale of Scones and Scoundrels

Deborah Garner

Cranberry Cove Press

Cranberry Bluff
by Deborah Garner

First Printing – November 2014
ISBN: 978-0-9960449-2-9

Printed in the U.S.A.

Also by Deborah Garner

Above the Bridge
The Moonglow Cafe

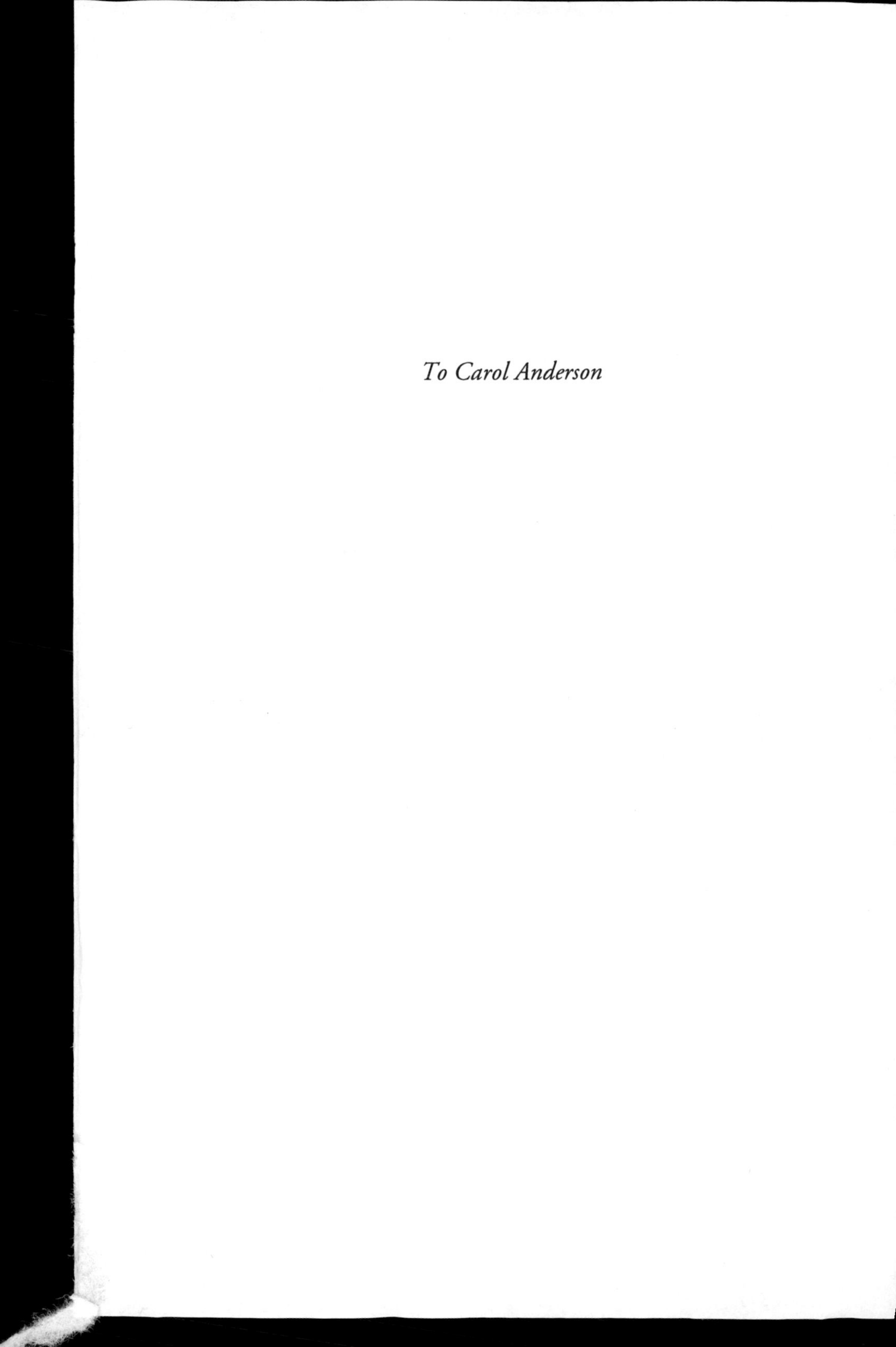

To Carol Anderson

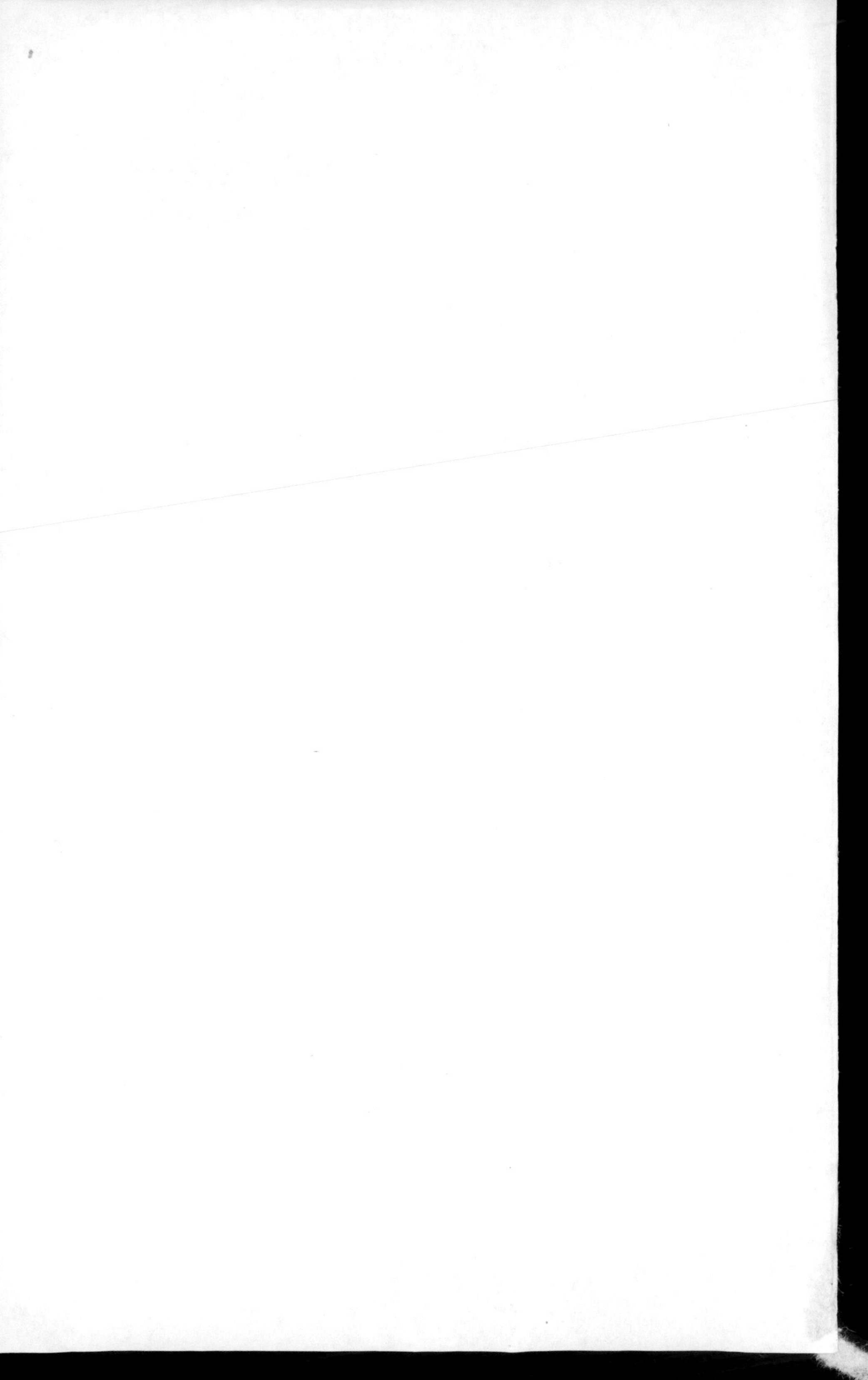

CHAPTER ONE

Molly Elliott plucked a cranberry jellybean from a crystal bowl in the parlor and looked out the front window. Fog hovered above the town, smothering shingled rooftops and beheading water towers. It was a typical morning along the Northern California coast, just as subdued as the day would be. Nothing ever happened in Cranberry Cove.

If things hadn't turned out so badly, she would have stayed in Florida. The humidity had been a drawback, but at least most days guaranteed sunshine. Still, she had welcomed the chance to take over Cranberry Cottage Bed and Breakfast. Not that she was glad to see Aunt Maggie pass away, but she had inherited the quaint business at the perfect time. Staying in Tallahassee had felt too dangerous.

She stopped her train of thought before memories began to kick-start her anxiety. Turning away from the window, she headed for the hall closet. Daily tasks calmed her down. There were plenty of chores to tackle, too, with five guests booked for that night – one couple and three singles. Four of the inn's eight rooms needed to be ready by mid-afternoon.

Aunt Maggie had taken reservations online, finding it easier than handling phone calls. Molly had changed that. Bookings could only be made by phone now. Molly checked the answering machine several times a day, selectively returning calls. She'd always had good instincts. The arriving guests had all been clear of red flags.

The Jensens, coming in from Boston, were a honeymoon couple. Molly smiled, remembering the excitement in the young bride's voice when she made the reservation. Their plans involved flying into San Francisco and taking a leisurely drive up the coast, stopping along the way in small towns and ending up in Seattle. The newlyweds would stay in the Cottage Suite, an elegant accommodation set in a renovated barn behind the main house. The antique four-poster bed, river rock fireplace and private hot tub on the suite's enclosed patio were perfect for a romantic stay. Molly made a mental note to put a vase of long-stemmed roses in the room, as well as imported chocolates on each pillow.

Not nearly as luxurious or spacious, but equally appropriate, the River Room would be ideal for Mr. Miller, a salesman from Bakersfield. He'd requested an accommodation with a desk and good lighting. That would cover his needs for writing up orders for the local business's office supplies. The hunter green décor and cherry wood furniture suited a single man, as did the old fishing equipment displayed on the walls. The banker's lamp on the desk cast a bright light. Charlie Miller's voice had been clear and precise. The room would be a good match.

Sadie Kramer had been a little harder to read and Molly almost used her "I'm so sorry, but we're full that evening" speech. But the elderly woman's voice pulled at Molly's heartstrings. Plus she had to hand it to the woman, traveling alone as a senior citizen. The guest reminded her of Aunt Maggie, who wouldn't have wanted her turned away. The cozy Battenberg Room would fit this guest nicely, with its white lace dresser runner and cool, blue bedding. The ground floor room would give Ms. Kramer easy access, plus the bay window offered a sitting area and partial ocean view.

Bryce Winslow would be the other guest checking in that evening. As much as Molly hated to admit it, his rich voice and suave manner on the phone had charmed her immediately. He'd asked for the best view available, not bothering to question prices. That was an easy request for Molly to fill. She had a weakness for smooth-talking men with big egos and big wallets, a type she knew well. The red and navy themed Lighthouse Room had an exquisite ocean view and was conveniently located at the very front of the bed and breakfast on the second floor, farthest from her innkeeper's room behind the kitchen. Temptation was the last thing she needed, especially of the male variety.

Molly looked at the clock and calculated a schedule for the day's work – beds made by noon, bath amenities and finishing touches done by one o'clock. A local maid service handled deep cleaning after checkouts, so that kept the list shorter than it might have been. She'd had no guests the night before, so that saved her having to work around their crew. She'd make a round of last-minute room checks by two, in case anything needed touching up.

A batch of scones – cranberry, of course – needed to be prepared and popped in the oven by three o'clock. That would take care of partial breakfast preparations, as well as filling the inn with the welcoming aroma of baked goods. She'd use a favorite recipe from Aunt Maggie's "Cranberry Cottage Cookbook," a short collection of recipes. Her aunt had always sent a copy home with each guest at checkout, a tradition Molly had continued. At four o'clock she'd set out a tray of imported cheese with English Water Crackers, accompanied by a selection of Napa Valley wines. She made another note to herself – check Aunt Maggie's crystal wine glasses for water spots.

List prepared, she pulled a broom from the closet and moved to the front porch. Grey clouds hovered above, casting shadows that warned of an eminent change in the weather.

It wasn't easy to keep the entrance tidy in September. Wind swept in off the ocean with a pestering regularity, rustling golden leaves off branches and scattering them on the ground. As soon as she collected one batch, another fluttered down into its place. On rainy days, leaves stuck to the roof like scraps of flypaper, weaving into the old Victorian's gingerbread trim. From the top of a ladder, Molly would pry them out by hand and toss them aside, leaving her palms and fingertips slick with grime. Climbing back down, she'd gather them into one soppy heap and shovel them into a wheelbarrow, moving them to a compost bin behind the building.

It was easier on days like this, when the air was dry and still. She could quickly sweep the porch, bag the leaves and haul them away. A few forceful shakes dusted off the wicker furniture's cushions. A quick spray from a hose perked up the containers of primrose that lined the steps from the walkway. It took only a short time to spruce up the outside of the inn. "What a beautiful place!" guests would say as they arrived.

Which is not at all what happened on this particular day.

After Molly neatened the yard, checked the guest rooms and laid out cheese, crackers and wine, a sharp rap on the door signaled the first guest's arrival. In spite of the open door and welcome sign to usher guests in on their own, Charlie Miller stood on the front porch and tapped his knuckles against the doorframe until Molly appeared. A sullen man, he stood at attention, silent, briefcase in hand. His brown hair was parted low and combed to the opposite side of his head.

A toupee? A bad comb over? A pair of wire-rimmed glasses perched on his nose. If he hadn't spoken, she would have guessed he was a solicitor.

"I am Charlie Miller," he said. "I have a reservation tonight. Please show me to my room."

"I'm Molly. Welcome to Cranberry Cottage Bed and Breakfast." She motioned him in and handed him a registration card. Without putting his briefcase down, he pulled a fountain pen from his front jacket pocket, leaned forward and signed the form with precision. Straightening up, he returned the pen to his pocket and addressed Molly again.

"Please show me to my room," he repeated.

The River Room had been the perfect choice for him, Molly concluded, not that his expression showed any reaction one way or another. Situated on the second floor, at the far back of the inn, it was quiet and removed. She led him to the room and pointed out the closet, bath, light switches and heater. He placed his briefcase on the desk and turned to face her as she stepped back into the hallway.

"Thank you," he said. He took the room key from her and closed the door.

Returning to the main floor, Molly filed his registration card away in the office. Mr. Miller was not exactly a gracious and friendly man, but he was a paying guest; she would make his stay as pleasant as possible. She walked to the kitchen, poured a mug of coffee and looked over a frittata recipe for the next morning. Making a quick note to pick some basil from the herb garden, she set the recipe aside and checked her appearance in an oak mirror on the back of the kitchen door.

Her five foot five stature and thick brown hair were just two of many features she'd inherited from her mother. In fact, Molly bore such an uncanny resemblance to her that younger pictures of her mother were often mistaken for pictures of her. In addition, Aunt Maggie had been her mother's identical twin, which often turned family albums into fodder for guessing games. Which picture was of which sister? Or were the pictures of Molly?

Bending toward the mirror, she turned her head from side to side. She'd inherited her slender face and high cheekbones from her father's side of the family, along with a light sprinkling of freckles that had been the source of much teasing in elementary school. As Molly approached adulthood, she attempted to cover them with makeup. Now, in her late twenties, she felt they embellished her relatively simple features.

Stepping back, Molly adjusted the simple tortoise shell headband that kept her hair away from her face. Determining she looked presentable, she returned to her desk in the front alcove and waited for the other guests.

Sadie Kramer was the next to arrive, bustling through the entrance thirty minutes later. A plump woman in her mid-sixties, she wore a floral dress in fuchsia tones that clashed violently with her red, bouffant hair. Knitting needles stuck out of an oversized tote bag that hung from her left arm. A bit of yarn drizzled alongside. In contrast to the first guest, Sadie was outgoing and friendly, fawning over the inn's décor. She complimented Molly on everything from the vase of fresh snapdragons on the registration table to the soft jazz that flowed from overhead speakers. She wasted no time scurrying to the appetizer table, demonstrating uncanny dexterity as she wedged a Brie-covered cracker between her lips while pouring a glass of wine.

Had Molly been able to hear the effervescent personality in Sadie's voice on the phone, she might have put her in a more flamboyant room – the Tulip Room, for example, with its multi-colored throw pillows or the Bistro Room, with its wine-labeled wallpaper. But a last-minute switch would be difficult. The Battenberg Room would have to do, white lace and all.

"I love every inch of this place!" Sadie exclaimed. Her tote bag smacked the cheese and cracker tray as she twirled around, causing her knitting needles to click together. "Are there other guests staying here tonight?"

"Yes, a few," Molly said, reaching out to catch a wine glass that Sadie's elbow had nudged. She placed it back on the table. "Let me set the tote bag aside for you."

"No, dear, that won't be necessary." Sadie pulled the bag in closer to her side as she reached for another cracker. "I'll just have a couple more bites and then settle in for the evening." She flashed a bright smile at Molly.

Sadie embraced the Battenberg room eagerly; she gushed over its details with enthusiasm that equaled what she'd exhibited in the parlor. "What lovely trinkets! What sweet doilies! What an adorable miniature tea set!" The woman patted the quilted bedding with one hand, nodding in approval. Molly watched the wine sway in the glass Sadie still clutched in her other hand. Sadie poked her head in the bathroom and popped back out. "I love that claw foot tub! And who would have thought to put teapots on a shower curtain? It's delightful!"

Leaving the exuberant woman to get settled, Molly returned to the kitchen. She dumped the coffee in the sink and poured herself a glass of wine. It was going to be a long evening.

Twilight had fallen by the time the next guests arrived. Had Molly not already known from the bride's initial phone call, it would have been clear the Jensens were newlyweds. They stepped through the front door with fingers intertwined and rosy glows on their faces. Dan Jensen looked like a schoolboy, shuffling from one foot to the other. *Mid-twenties,* Molly thought, *married straight out of the home he grew up in.* Susan, who introduced herself as Susie, was petite and soft-spoken, with shoulder-length blonde hair held back with a pink headband. She lifted her free hand to wave a coy hello. *Barely out of her teens,* Molly assessed at first glance. *No,* she corrected herself, *mid-twenties with a young face.*

Dan signed his registration card with the dignified manner of a young man eager to show he was an adult. They'd booked a reservation for several nights and had suitcases to unload from their rental car but declined help. Molly handed them a key and pointed toward a cobblestone path, well lit by low garden lights shaped like tiny gnomes. They'd have no trouble finding the private Cottage Suite.

Molly closed the door and checked the grandfather clock in the hallway. Solid mahogany and six feet tall, it had been in the family for four generations. Shipped across the country three times during its lifetime, it bore only one tiny scratch that stain concealed.

Seven o'clock.

Molly loved the details of her daily routine as an innkeeper. Up by six each morning, she made a small pot of coffee for herself while a larger one brewed for guests. By six-thirty, she set out coffee, cream and sugar in the front hallway. She finished most preparations the night before – biscuit batter made, egg casseroles assembled, fresh fruit cut. She served simple but delicious, attractively presented homemade food, none of that complicated fare that looked great in magazines, but didn't always suit everyone's taste. She'd never win a spot on a cooking show with her philosophy, but guests always seemed pleased with her focus on a welcoming morning atmosphere.

Serving breakfast never felt like work. It was more like throwing a party, except the guests were sober. Usually, that is. Every now and then someone would stagger to the morning meal after a late night at Paddy's Pub House, not quite recovered. But a few cups of java down the pipe did a lot to improve that person's coherence. Most guests conversed with each other over their servings of cranberry pancakes or scrambled cheddar eggs. Molly enjoyed hearing stories of where the travelers had been or where they were headed next.

In the hour after breakfast, she cleaned up, washed dishes, said goodbye to departing guests and prepared for later arrivals. Sometimes a day would pop up with no stay-overs and no incoming guests. Those days were rare, but freeing. Molly would set up a couple of rooms "just in case," check the answering machine and head out to walk on the beach. She both loved and dreaded those particular days. The Pacific Ocean breeze was misty and cool, a refreshing change from the heat of Florida. But the free time also had a down side. Memories knocked against her mind, demanding to enter. Usually she could fight them off, but not always.

The ringing phone snapped Molly out of her reverie. She set her wine glass down and moved to the answering machine. Perhaps the last guest was calling to say he was on his way? But no, it was a request for a reservation the following month – two couples traveling together, asking for two rooms. The Starboard Room and the Port Room could be combined with an intersecting sitting area to form the Captain's Suite, a perfect set-up for friends who wanted to visit, but still wanted privacy. Molly returned the phone call, marked the reservation on the inn's calendar and checked the time.

Eight o'clock.

Technically, check-in time ranged from four in the afternoon to eight in the evening. But life didn't always go according to plan, as Molly knew. The drive up the coast from San Francisco was winding and difficult to navigate after dark. On a map, it appeared shorter than it actually was. Guests often ended up apologizing for late arrivals they didn't anticipate.

She returned to the parlor and picked up the cheese and cracker tray with one hand, grabbing the open bottle of wine with the other. The last guest would have to settle for one of the cranberry white chocolate chip bars that she set out at night.

Molly heard footsteps from the hallway, and Sadie appeared, wine glass in hand. She'd changed from her earlier dress into black slacks and an emerald green cashmere sweater – a much better compliment to her red hair, Molly thought. Then again, who was she to determine what people should wear?

"Such delicious wine!" Sadie said, extending her empty glass.

"It's a Chardonnay from Napa Valley, one of my personal favorites." Molly poured Sadie a refill. The woman helped herself to more crackers and started back to her room, shrugging her shoulders in a "thank you" gesture as she started down the hall.

Molly put away the cheese, crackers and wine and replaced them with the plate of baked treats. She looked over the remaining guest card, checking for any notes about late arrival. There were none. She skimmed the reservation book for incoming guests the next few nights. The book was clear of arrivals. It would be an easy weekend – no rooms turning over. Sadie Kramer was scheduled to check out on Tuesday. Mr. Miller had indicated he was there for either two or three nights, depending on his travel plans. The Jensens were there for several nights. And Bryce Winslow.... Molly paused.

She'd placed a question mark in the departure date on his registration. Had his charm distracted her so much that she overlooked this detail? It wasn't like her to get rattled easily. At least she never used to.

Setting the paperwork aside, she made sure the front porch lights were on. A strong wind had started to kick up and Molly could feel rain in the air. She straightened the welcome mat and closed the door quickly.

She pulled a current paperback bestseller from the parlor bookshelf and curled up on the couch, hoping the book would interest her more than the last time she tried to read it. She took another glance at the stately mahogany clock before turning to the book's first page.

Eight forty-five.

Molly heard the front door open. *Finally,* she thought, putting the book down and heading to the entrance.

Susie Jensen stood there, her feet swathed in white and pink terrycloth, an empty ice bucket in her hand. *Seriously, bunny slippers?*

"I'm sorry, I hope I'm not intruding," Susie said. "I didn't see an ice machine out back." The young woman's smile struck Molly as fragile.

"I'll fill it for you in the kitchen," Molly said. "And, no, you're not intruding at all. The parlor is always open to guests. Once all the guests have arrived, I do lock the door at night. But that second key on your key ring will let you in." Her words floated back over her shoulder as she went into the kitchen.

"Oh!" The young guest seemed surprised. "I thought it was a duplicate, since there are two of us." The sound of tumbling ice drowned out the comment.

"Your suite is the only accommodation that's separate from the main house," Molly explained as she returned with a full ice bucket.

Susie took the ice from Molly and thanked her. She turned and left through the front door, rabbit ears flopping with each step. Light raindrops began to fall as Susie followed the cobblestone walkway around the house. A strong gust of wind rattled the wind chimes on the porch. Molly shivered and closed the door, glancing again at the clock.

Ten thirty.

At this point, Molly was equally worried and annoyed. The confirmation sheet that she sent to guests clearly indicated check-in hours and stated guests should call ahead if they would be late so that she could arrange for their arrival. There weren't enough dead cell phone areas along the coast to force an innkeeper to spend a night curled up on the couch for hours, waiting for a late guest. Yet hours passed without a call. Molly fought to stay awake, still disinterested in the paperback. But as the storm grew more intense, pattering raindrops lulled her to sleep.

CHAPTER TWO

A pounding on the door woke Molly. She sat up, disoriented, as the paperback she'd been trying to read slid off her chest and landed on the floor. She rubbed her eyes and looked at the clock.

Midnight.

Had she imagined the sound? She picked up the book and set it on a side table, then reconsidered and put it back on the bookshelf. If it hadn't caught her attention by now, it wasn't going to.

A steady knocking, sounding louder than the pounding that woke her, confirmed that the last guest had arrived. Finally, she could check him in and retire to her room. She flung the door open and caught her breath.

The tall man who stood on the front porch could have walked straight out of a romance novel, with his dark hair plastered to his forehead, tanned, chiseled features and coffee-colored eyes. He wore a tailored business suit that looked like it had just been pulled from a washing machine. A suitcase sat beside him, wet airline tag blowing sideways with each gust of wind.

He cleared his throat. "May I come in?"

Warmth crept up Molly's neck. Yes, that was the voice she'd heard on the phone when the reservation was made. His voice was gorgeous. So was he.

Molly snapped out of her daze and motioned him in out of the storm. "Of course! I'm so sorry, please come in." She'd forgotten her annoyance over his late arrival, at least until she noticed his share of rain dripping off his trousers and onto the floor. Bryce ran a damp sleeve across his forehead, realizing immediately that it did nothing to dry off his skin.

"Let me get you something to help dry off." Molly slipped into the hallway's guest bath and retrieved a deep burgundy plush hand towel.

Bryce dried his face and hands, cleared his throat and glanced around. "Did I wake you?" His confused expression clashed with his otherwise attractive demeanor.

Molly managed a simultaneous sigh and smile. Honestly, not even an apology for arriving so late? This was one of many reasons she'd jumped at the chance to take over the B&B. City folk took so much for granted.

"Our check-in hours are usually from four to eight, Mr. Winslow," Molly said. "But it's no problem. I'm glad you made it safely. If I'd known a storm was coming in when you made your reservation I would have warned you about the long drive up here. It's not too bad on a sunny day, but a rainy night is another story altogether." *Why was she chattering all of a sudden?*

"I assumed the registration desk was open late."

Molly didn't reply. A city hotel might have a round-the-clock front desk, but a bed and breakfast wouldn't. What was this guy doing way up in Cranberry Cove, anyway? He should have booked a room in San Francisco and saved himself hours of driving, not to mention a dry cleaning bill.

She handed him a pen and pointed to the registration card on the hallway table.

"Let's get you into your room," Molly said. "I'm sure you're tired, not to mention anxious to get into dry clothes."

She watched as he signed the form with a bold, self-assured movement. Moisture covered his steady, well-manicured hand. This was not a man who did manual labor. And certainly not one who was accustomed to driving winding coastal roads at night.

"Ocean view room, I believe," Bryce said, picking up the suitcase. A trickle of water ran off onto the floor.

"Not at night," Molly quipped, catching the guest off-guard.

"What?" he said.

"We only have ocean view rooms in the daytime," Molly said as she turned toward the stairs with his room key. She heard a light laugh behind her. "Follow me, Mr. Winslow. Your room is upstairs and to the right."

"Call me Bryce." His footsteps echoed hers.

"It's our largest room, aside from the suite in the back building."

"Oh, you have a suite? Well then, I'll take that, instead." Molly heard the footsteps stop. She continued without looking back.

"Mr. Winslow…"

"Call me Bryce…"

"Bryce," Molly said. "The suite is already occupied, and besides, it has no ocean view, which is what you requested."

"Not even in the daytime?"

She turned to face him as they reached the door to the Lighthouse Room, finding him only inches from her. She stumbled a little. For the first time since he'd arrived, he was smiling. Grinning would be a better description, she thought.

Yes, a smug grin. The kind that should come with a warning sign, since trouble usually accompanied it.

"No, *Bryce*," Molly said, emphasizing his name, "not even in the daytime." She smiled, but suppressed a full grin. She wasn't going to fall for the charm, was she? She had sworn off his type years ago.

"You'll find everything you need in your room," Molly said.

"Dry towels?" Another grin.

"Yes, dry towels," Molly answered, fighting back a laugh. "Breakfast is served downstairs from eight o'clock to ten o'clock."

"I don't eat breakfast."

What man doesn't eat breakfast?

"Feel free to help yourself to coffee then, any time after six-thirty, in the front hallway." Molly handed him the room key, said goodnight and started back downstairs.

"See you at breakfast."

"I thought…." Molly paused on the stairs. She could picture his grin without turning around.

"I was kidding."

The door to the Lighthouse Room closed.

****

It was nearly one in the morning and Molly was barely into her flannel nightshirt. Her alarm would be ringing in five hours. Worse, now she was wide awake. That book! If that book had been the least bit interesting, it might have kept her awake until Mr. Winslow – Bryce! – arrived, and she wouldn't be awake now.

Who was she kidding? She wasn't irritated at the book. It was that arrogant, smug, inconsiderate, self-obsessed…. She was running out of adjectives! But Mr. Winslow – Bryce! – had all the traits that she tried to avoid in men. His late, unapologetic arrival alone was rude, and now it would take her an hour to get to sleep and three cups of coffee to wake up in five hours.

She checked the alarm on the nightstand clock and flopped down on the bed. She closed her eyes. They popped right back open. Closed them again, opened them again and sat up. *Still awake!*

He reminded her of Franco, a foreign exchange student she'd dated in high school. That was more years ago than she cared to count. But Franco's classic Italian features and lady-killer demeanor were still freshly imprinted in her mind. No question, it had been exhilarating to loop her arm through his while he carried her books through the school hallways. She'd been the envy of half the senior class whenever he'd cast his sexy eyes sideways at her. His return to Italy had been her first real heartbreak, which was compounded by his broken promises to write. She never heard from him again.

That should have been enough for her to steer clear of handsome smooth talkers. But it wasn't. Ron in grad school, for example, had smothered her with affection – between clandestine visits to his other girlfriends. And Harrison, a big shot manager at one of her first jobs. She'd been flattered that he'd taken her under his wing to help her career, plying her with roses and romantic dinners. That ended on a bad note when she caught him in bed with a sexy new hire. No, she wasn't going to reminisce about past relationships. She had five mouths to feed in the morning and needed to sleep. She forced herself to mentally prepare the breakfast, her own version of counting sheep. *Pre-heat the oven. Grind the French roast beans and start the coffee maker. Fill goblets with fresh melon and berries. Slide the mushroom and cheese frittata into the oven. Double-check the place settings in the breakfast room…*

CHAPTER THREE

Sadie was the first to arrive at breakfast, not at all a surprise. She looked well rested, Molly thought, though compared to the way Molly felt, anyone would. It had been nearly two in the morning before she'd been able to fall asleep.

The lemon colored jogging suit Sadie wore added warmth to the table, which was otherwise framed by a picture window displaying the town's usual morning fog. With a touch of luck they'd get sunshine in the afternoon, but Molly wasn't betting on it.

"What a beautiful table arrangement!" Sadie exclaimed. Molly stifled a yawn and thanked her, setting a cup of honeydew melon and blackberries in front of the smiling woman. A mint leaf garnished the dish. She set an identical cup at each place setting.

"Where did you get such a gorgeous china set?" Sadie asked.

"From my Aunt Maggie," Molly said. "It was her inn before she passed away. I inherited the belongings, as well as the inn."

Sadie scooped a spoonful of fresh berries into her mouth, closed her eyes, swallowed and sighed.

"Well, you can't go wrong with this type of pattern," she said. "Petite flowers and gold trim are so elegant – very

English, if I may be so bold." Sadie tried, poorly, to mimic a British accent. "My mother had a pattern like this, except with different flowers and a silver trim. I just love the gold!"

Molly left Sadie to admire the place settings and finish her fruit. When she returned with two baskets of cranberry scones, Mr. Miller had joined Sadie, who was trying to start a conversation with him. It was clear she wasn't making much progress.

Molly placed a basket of scones at each end of the table and picked up a coffee pot from a warming tray on a side table.

"Coffee for you, Mr. Miller?" Molly asked. Receiving no answer, she poured the beverage into the man's coffee mug, watching for a response. "Thank you," he said, without looking up. Molly watched Sadie eye him curiously. *My reaction, exactly*, she thought.

"So, where are you from, Mr. Miller?" Sadie reached for a cranberry scone, knocking over a saltshaker in the process. She pinched salt from the table with her fingers. "Can't ever be too careful!" she said.

Mr. Miller frowned as he watched Sadie throw salt over her left shoulder. "Bakersfield," he replied.

Sadie nodded as she broke the scone in half and slathered the middle with butter. Mr. Miller frowned again.

"Bakersfield," Sadie repeated. "I've never been there. It's small, right?"

"Not really," he said. He shook his head as Molly offered him a scone. He sipped his coffee.

"I'm from San Francisco," Sadie said. "I don't know how I'd survive in a little place like Bakersfield, though I'm sure it's charming!" She beamed at Mr. Miller, who stared back blankly. "I love the hustle and bustle of the city! We have so many fabulous stores, though I suppose you're not much of a shopper, Mr. Miller." She paused for a response, getting none. "And the museums and shows – there's always something to do! A person could never be bored in San Francisco. Why just last week...."

Sadie continued her ravings about San Francisco life while Molly slid hot plates of frittata in front of both guests. Mr. Miller didn't refuse the food, but didn't pick up his fork. Sadie attacked it immediately. "Delicious!" she said.

The Jensens entered the dining room with fingers intertwined, just as they had been when they checked in. Susie had the bright, beaming look of a high school cheerleader.

"I hope you slept well," Molly said.

"We did!" Susie looked shyly at Dan, who kissed her hand.

"Mr. Miller," Molly addressed the silent man, "these are two of my other guests, Dan and Susie Jensen. Dan and Susie, this is Mr. Charlie Miller."

"Nice to meet you," Susie said. Mr. Miller sighed into his plate and didn't acknowledge the introduction.

"Have a seat," Molly told the young couple.

Susie smiled coyly as she requested breakfast to go. Dan stood obediently by her side in a way that only a henpecked husband in training could.

"Absolutely, it'll be no problem at all." Molly retreated to the kitchen and returned with two more frittata servings. She motioned to the basket of scones on the table.

"How was your evening?" Molly asked. "Did you find one of the local cafés?"

"We did," Dan answered as he added cranberry scones to the plates. "It was called...what was it called, again, sweetheart?" He directed his question to Susie.

"Eleanor's," Susie said. "Just a couple blocks down the road. It was very good."

"That's one of my favorites," Molly said. It was actually her absolute favorite. Eleanor Merkin had been a fixture in Cranberry Cove for decades. Molly had heard Aunt Maggie rave about Eleanor's cooking many times. It had been an obsession of her aunt's to find out Eleanor's recipe for chicken potpie. She'd never succeeded. Molly had always hoped Eleanor would publish a cookbook with her recipes. It was a good bet that it would sell well with customers of the much-loved café.

"Oh, I love that place! I try to go at least once every time I come to Cranberry Cove. Eleanor is such a dear," Sadie exclaimed. "What did you order? Appetizer? Salad? Entrée? Dessert? Do tell!"

"We had...what did we have, sweetheart?" Dan deferred to Susie, who detailed their order perfectly.

"Stuffed mushrooms for appetizer, cranberry kale salad, roast turkey with cranberry relish for Dan, pasta with a pesto sauce for me, and cranberry pear walnut cobbler with vanilla bean ice cream for dessert." Susie gave Dan an adoring look as she recited the meal choices.

"It sounds divine!" Sadie grabbed another scone. "I must go there tonight. Maybe you'd like to go, too, Mr. Miller?"

"I don't think so," he said. He stood, set his fork at a diagonal angle across his plate and pushed in his chair. He bowed slightly in Molly's direction and left the room.

Odd little man, Molly thought as she watched him walk away.

Susie thanked Molly and pulled Dan out through the breakfast room's French doors. The two disappeared down the side pathway as quickly as they had arrived.

She checked her watch. Another thirty minutes remained for breakfast service. Four guests had been fed, which left just one more to go: Mr. "Call me Bryce" Winslow, of course. He'd probably slide in at the last minute, she thought as she stepped back into the kitchen for more coffee.

As if to defy her, she heard Bryce Winslow enter the room at that moment. He greeted Sadie, introducing himself. "How nice to meet you, Sadie – quite a becoming color you're wearing there!"

"Why, Mr. Winslow, what a sweet thing to say!" Sadie let out a flattered laugh befitting a woman half her age. At least she had spirit.

"Please, call me Bryce."

"Bryce it is, then." Another laugh.

Out of view, Molly rolled her eyes. At least Sadie was still there in the breakfast room. Molly wouldn't have to converse with him alone. Sadie could keep the conversation going herself, as could Bryce, she suspected.

Molly emerged from the kitchen with Bryce's breakfast plate and a fresh pot of coffee. She paused. A new, vastly improved model replaced the dripping, rain-soaked man who had arrived so late. His hair, now dry, was a lighter brown than it had appeared the night before. His casual sweater didn't hide his muscular build the way his wet suit had.

Bryce met Molly's gaze as she approached him, and his eyes sparkled under the overhead light.

"Don't mind if I do," he said, picking up his coffee cup and holding it out. She felt herself blush as she filled his cup. Freshly showered and shaved, he wore a faint trace of cologne. What was that scent? Something woodsy and invigorating.

"And how is our lovely innkeeper this morning?" He smiled brightly at Molly.

Sadie jumped in. "She *is* lovely, don't you think? I was so relieved when I arrived yesterday. Some innkeepers are just plain insufferable. Oops! Not nice to say so, I know. But it's always a relief to know your host or hostess is welcoming. Makes a place feel like home, even if it's only for a short time."

"Indeed it does," Bryce said. "Feels just like home." His gaze never wavered, and Molly's discomfort grew.

"Actually, I'm a little tired today," Molly said, directing the comment to Sadie. She smiled to tone down the passive-aggressive jab after it slipped out. Bryce hadn't arrived late on purpose, after all.

"Well, that's understandable, dear," Sadie said. "I'm sure keeping this place running is a lot of work. And you manage so well all alone. It's gorgeous and so inviting!" She finished a last bite of frittata and set her fork down, exhaling. A satisfied smile spread across her face.

"Sadie's right," Bryce said. "This must be a lot of work. I hope you're able to get enough rest."

Molly fought back the urge to look at Bryce. She could tell by the tone of his voice that he was teasing her. "Usually I do," she said.

"Oh, my!" Sadie glanced at her rhinestone wristwatch and jumped up. "Stores are opening already. You must excuse me. My favorite part of coming up to Cranberry Cove is the shopping! So many quaint things we don't see in the city." She pushed her chair in and left the room, her hand waving above her head. "Have a good day, everyone!"

"Wine and cheese at five o'clock," Molly called after Sadie. She exhaled, nervous. Now only Bryce remained at the table. She removed Sadie's plate and started for the kitchen.

"Ah, it's later than I thought," Bryce said. That amazing voice caught her before she made it out of the room. "The breakfast hours are over. I don't want to hold up your morning." There was no way to avoid him. Molly did an about-face. Bryce folded his cloth napkin and set it on the table.

"Oh, don't worry – take your time," Molly said. "No rush. Checkout's not until eleven."

"Well, in that case I can really take my time. I'm not checking out today." Bryce flashed another bright smile.

Molly paused, remembering the question mark on his registration card. How had she managed to take a reservation without noting the departure date? It was a good thing there was no one else checking into that room on the day's schedule. She could extend the booking another night.

"Right," she said quickly. "You check out on...." With luck, he would fill in the blank.

"Next week, I believe," Bryce said.

"Next...week...?" Molly tried to keep her response from sounding like a question, but was unsuccessful. She barely kept the panic out of her voice. How was she going to deal with him for a whole week? She could hardly focus as it was. She took Sadie's plate into the kitchen and returned to fill up Bryce's coffee.

"Yes, next week," Bryce repeated. He turned down the refill. "Isn't that what your records say? I'm sure that's what I reserved."

"I'm sure that's right," Molly said quickly. "I just don't always have dates in my head. I should go check the inn's register." She cringed inside at the lame excuse to leave the room.

Bryce stood. Again Molly fought to stay calm and detached. His casual khakis revealed a trim waistline.

"Thank you for breakfast." Bryce smiled once more before leaving the room. Molly watched him walk down the inn's hallway and listened to his footsteps on the stairs. Only when she heard his guest room door close did she start back to the kitchen.

CHAPTER FOUR

Susie followed Sadie into The Closet Collection, a cozy boutique in the center of Cranberry Cove's historic district. Racks of women's clothing lined both walls, sorted by color and size. Susie thought this was an odd way of organizing a store. If a customer liked blue and wore a medium, anything she might want would be in one section – blouses, pants, jackets, sweaters, even shoes. For the heftier purple-lover, an equally abundant yet consolidated section could be found elsewhere. Susie was used to boutiques being organized by type of clothing article: all sweaters in one area, all skirts in another.

"This is my favorite store," Sadie said. Her enthusiasm was evident as she browsed from rack to rack, starting with reds and moving right down the line to browns. She gathered up a dozen hangers of assorted items and headed for the back of the shop. "This is where you mix your colors!" she exclaimed as she latched her dressing room door.

Susie bypassed the clothing racks and headed for a glass case of jewelry. Pendants of semi-precious stones and crystals spread across shelving inside. Earrings and bracelets dangled from circular racks above. Susie lifted a card from one of the racks, holding a pair of pearl studs against one ear lobe. With her other hand, she shifted the remaining earring holders on the rack so they hung evenly, without spaces between the cards. Heading for the ivory section of the store, she flipped through a row of sweaters, finding a sweet cardigan with tiny pearls for buttons. *Perfect,* she thought. *And an excellent match for…* she moved to a corner display of clothing and pulled an elegant pair of beige slacks from a waterfall display. Yes, that would make a good combination and would go well with the earrings. She checked the price tags of all three items – a little expensive, but that wouldn't be a problem.

"How does this look?" Sadie's voice boomed across the sales floor as she stepped out of the dressing room. She wore a ruffled blouse in fire engine red, along with a flowing skirt in bright purple. Noting Susie's raised eyebrows, she explained, "Red Hat Society! Meetings every month. I have to make a fashion statement at the events, you know." She popped back into the dressing room.

Moving around the store, Susie picked up an emerald T-shirt, snug blue jeans and a lacey beige camisole, matching that with a sparkling bracelet of multicolored beads and crystals. A third and fourth outfit chosen, she joined Sadie in the dressing room area, picking a space two stalls down.

"What did you find?" Sadie shouted. Susie heard a clattering of hangers.

"Cute stuff!" Susie replied, her voice cheerful. *Not really,* she thought to herself.

A third voice entered the conversation. "Are you finding everything you need?" a salesgirl asked. "Should I bring other colors or sizes?"

"I'm fine," Susie said. Her muffled voice carried through the camisole she was pulling over her head.

"Nothing needed here," Sadie added. "Everything is fabulous! This is my favorite store in Cranberry Cove!"

"Delighted to hear that," the salesgirl said. "I'll check back in a little bit, just in case you need anything."

"Thank you," Susie and Sadie said simultaneously.

Susie worked her way through the outfits, while chatting with Sadie over the thin, dressing room walls. Once Sadie left and headed for the sales counter, Susie gathered her choices and left the dressing room, circling the store to replace some of the items on racks while the salesgirl was ringing up Sadie's purchases.

As Sadie gathered her items, Susie set the ivory sweater on the counter.

"Excellent choice," the salesgirl said. "I love the pearl buttons down the front. I have this same sweater – couldn't resist it when the shipment came in." She lowered her voice and bent forward as she removed the security sensor from the sweater. "I love working here because we get to see everything UPS delivers. We get first choice – and an employee discount." She glanced around as she admitted this, which Susie found ridiculous, since there weren't any other sales clerks or customers in the store.

Wrapping the sweater in tissue paper, the girl slid it into a sturdy paper bag with the store's name and logo on the front. She handed it to Susie with a smile. "Enjoy!"

"I plan to," Susie responded with enthusiasm. Though it didn't equal Sadie's glee, it was enough to satisfy the salesgirl.

Sadie was waiting on the sidewalk, holding several bags. Susie trailed her through an artisan co-op, a yarn shop, a shoe boutique, two jewelry stores and three other clothing establishments. Sadie left each location with a new batch of purchases. Susie bought an item or two at some of the stores, nothing at others.

"Newlywed budget," she said as Sadie eyed her small collection of bags. "I try to buy only a few things each time I shop."

"Widow's wealth!" Sadie laughed, barely able to juggle the massive number of bags she held. "Time to drop these off at the inn. I must free my arms up for more shopping later!" She bustled down the sidewalk with Susie following.

CHAPTER FIVE

Molly dried the last of the breakfast dishes and put them away before sitting down to look over the inn's schedule. No new arrivals were due that evening, or the next. But she had to do some shuffling to accommodate Bryce Winslow's longer stay. She still couldn't believe she hadn't written down his departure date. That wasn't like her. She always kept on top of the details in her reservation book. Had their phone conversation thrown her off-balance that much? Apparently it had.

She didn't like feeling scattered, the way she'd felt when she left Tallahassee. Taking over Aunt Maggie's bed and breakfast in Cranberry Cove had been a chance for her to reorganize her life, to start over. It was one of the main reasons she was there.

Molly shuddered, thinking about Florida. Her life there had been peaceful for so many years. She'd loved her job as an administrative assistant at a small advertising agency. Long work hours during the week were rewarded with free weekends. She didn't have to put in the extra hours that the ad execs did. Saturdays and Sundays often found her enjoying the warm waters on a Gulf Coast beach or adventuring through swamp areas. She'd landed some impressive alligator pictures on one of those trips.

Her duties at the ad agency were basic, which suited her just fine. She handled incoming phone calls, made coffee, kept appointment calendars updated and ran errands when needed. Aside from the lack of romance in her life, it was a perfect existence. Until that day.

She hadn't realized at the time that she'd walked into a bad situation. It was an ordinary morning. She'd stopped at FedEx to send out an overnight package, chatting about sports with the clerk, a college student. He was a Gators fan; she was a Seminoles fan. They had a long history of jovial teasing whenever she dropped off shipments.

From the FedEx office she'd stopped at a favorite coffee house, grabbing a decaf macchiato to go. Her next stop was a quick drive-through at the post office, where she dropped a batch of metered mailings in the driveway box. And then she went to the bank.

For the three years she'd worked for the ad agency, she'd taken a daily deposit to the bank. She was a stickler for accuracy, and the execs appreciated her efficient loyalty. She never thought twice about her quick jaunts in and out of the bank building. It was an errand, just like any other errand she had to run. At least it was, until the day a woman at the teller's window next to her pulled out a gun. One minute Molly was thanking the teller for the ad agency's deposit receipt. The next, she was sprawled out on the floor, like everyone else who had the misfortune to be in the bank at that moment.

It had all happened so quickly, though it didn't seem like that at the time. The news reports later would say the robber was gone within six minutes. To Molly, face pressed against the bank's cold, marble floor, it felt like hours.

That should have been the end of it. The whole episode should have gone down as a terrifying close call. She could have gone on with her life as it had been if not for a wild twist of fate. The robber had the same build, hair length and hair color as Molly, who had walked away quickly after the incident even before police arrived. She was shaken, but assumed the experience was over. Little did she know what was about to unfold.

Molly had never been much of a television watcher. She didn't turn on the news automatically when she walked in her apartment from work. That evening when she arrived home, her phone had been ringing, but she was exhausted from the trauma of the day and let it go to voicemail. So to say she was in shock when the police showed up at her door that evening would be an understatement. Had she been following the newscasts, she would have seen the photos being compared: the one from the teller window next to her, the one from the teller window where she was.

Of course, she was cleared, after being dragged down to the police station and questioned for hours. Both tellers verified that she was not the robber. The security camera on the opposite side of the building showed her walking to her car, not running in the opposite direction. Close examination indicated that her hair was approximately one inch longer than the thief's hair. She was at least an inch shorter, one deputy said, though there wasn't a clear shot of the robber's shoes. And her weight was about ten pounds heavier, another added, which had caused Molly to frown. No more late night snacking, she vowed.

It should have all ended there, but it didn't. The first few days were fine, in fact, almost fun. She was an office celebrity, the one who'd nabbed primetime television coverage without even needing to run an ad. Friends she hadn't heard from for ages called to ask her out for coffee or lunch. Her neighbors brought over baskets of muffins. One boy rode by on a bike, waving and calling out, "I saw you on TV!"

And then the notes began to arrive; cutout letters glued to pieces of paper contained the threatening messages. She found the first one under her front doormat, short and to the point. "We know you're the one." The second landed in her mailbox, stating, "You won't get away with it." The third one sent her over the edge: "We want the money back." That started the chills running up her spine.

Morning commutes had been leisurely drives before the bank robbery. Now they became paranoid trips with Molly checking the rearview mirror all the time. Grocery shopping felt dangerous; every passing customer made her nervous. Who was sending her the notes? It could have been anyone. Each person she ran into was suspect. She began to dread going out in public.

Her anxiety heightened when she came home from work one day to find her front door ajar, her apartment ransacked. The contents of drawers had been dumped on the floor and her closet was a mess. Another note of choppy, glued letters was left on her kitchen table, saying, "We will find it."

She contacted the police, changed her locks and secured her windows, but it wasn't enough to keep panic attacks at bay. Sleep was elusive and the tiniest noise sent her nerves careening. She couldn't eat, couldn't function at work and began staying away from home as much as possible, grabbing motel rooms or spending weekends out of town. The police had no leads.

She started seeing a therapist to work on anxiety issues, but that proved useless, as well. The therapist helped as someone to talk to, but it didn't solve the basic problem: someone was after her.

Nothing remained of the life she'd established in Tallahassee. She distrusted the people around her, becoming suspicious of everyone from her co-workers to the police officers handling the case. Was her therapist in on it? Was the grocery clerk watching her? Were the police starting to suspect she was actually guilty? Were her friends really friends? The constant paranoia suffocated her.

And then Aunt Maggie passed away. Unmarried and childless, her aunt had left her California bed and breakfast to Molly in her will. Molly knew her mother's twin sister had always considered her the daughter she never had. She had fond childhood memories of spending summer vacations in Cranberry Cove with Aunt Maggie, who told stories of how the town had attempted to grow cranberries, but found it wasn't as successful as it was for towns farther north, in southern Oregon. The cranberry bogs were gone, but the name "Cranberry Cove" had stuck, which was a good move for tourism. A visitor could hardly turn in any direction without running into cranberry something-or-other.

Although Molly hadn't visited often as an adult, she'd always kept in touch with Aunt Maggie, first through hand-written letters and, later, through email. That had been something – convincing her elderly aunt to get a computer and email account!

After the bank robbery, taking over the bed and breakfast was a chance for Molly to escape, to move three thousand miles away and start a new life. She packed her bags and left in the middle of the night, bought a one-way train ticket to safety. Occasionally she still glanced over her shoulder or jumped when the telephone rang. But the threatening notes never followed her, and the guests at the inn were always pleasant. She'd kept no contact with any co-workers in Florida. Sometimes she missed the life she'd had in

Tallahassee, the comfort of a longtime routine. But she never missed the daily fear.

CHAPTER SIX

Dan was stretched out on the bed in the Cottage Suite, flipping through a local travel magazine when Susie walked in. "All ads," he criticized. "I don't know why travelers even bother to read these things."

He tossed the magazine aside. "So, how did you do today? A decent haul?"

"Not great." Susie tossed her bags on the sofa in the sitting area. "Some pearl earrings, a lace camisole, a rhinestone bracelet and a scarf from the local artist co-op. And a sweater that I actually paid for. I like the scarf."

"Sorry, dear. Not the cream of the crop selection you're used to." He patted the bed, inviting her to join him. "Maybe you need a new hobby."

"Don't start that 'dear' crap or get any ideas," Susie snapped. "It's bad enough I have to be affectionate to you inside the inn. Don't push it."

"All part of the job, sweetheart."

"You heard me. Zip it." Susie pulled the pearl earrings from her jacket pocket and tossed them on the table in front of the sofa. She dug the bracelet from the other pocket and the scarf from her oversized tote.

"There's a light out along the garden pathway," Dan said.

"Who cares?" Susie's tone was disgusted. "It's not like this is the Four Seasons." She reached into a shopping bag and pulled out other items.

"Ooh, let me see the camisole," Dan said.

"I told you, zip it." Susie dropped her jacket on the sofa and headed to the bathroom, closing the door. She took off her baggy sweater, pulled the camisole off her slender torso and folded it neatly.

"This town is beyond boring," she shouted through the door. "Even the stores are a drag. I miss Miami and New York and Chicago and Boston."

"Tough luck, honey," Dan said. "You're stuck here for the time being."

Susie threw the bathroom door open and glared at Dan.

"Listen, you low life. In the first place, I'm not your honey, sweetheart or dear. So lay off that crap when we're not in public. And second of all, if you hadn't decided to go after the reward money, I wouldn't be trapped in a tiny diorama of a town."

"Come on, it's not that bad, especially when we're going to split the reward."

"It's exactly that bad, and worse."

Susie's patience with Dan was growing thin. There were many other detectives out there who would have made more interesting fake husbands. Ralph, for example, was bright enough to add character to his roles. Or Jonathan, boring but loaded with cash. He never passed up fine dining and plentiful cocktails, and always footed the tab. Even better, Gregory, or whatever his real name was. Now there was a bonus partner – great conversationalist, great looking and one hell of a kisser. She'd pushed for more romance every time she'd been on assignment with him. But he'd always held back. He was a smart agent who didn't mix work with pleasure. That was a man she'd like to conquer in the future. Maybe she'd try to get hooked up with him again. She'd put in a request with the agencies he worked with.

She certainly wasn't about to go out on the road with Dan again, if she could help it. This time it had been convenient; she had an agenda of her own. But she was a free agent. She could do what she wanted. And spending time with Dan wasn't in her plans.

"I don't have to work with you, you know," she said. "There are plenty of detective agencies that offer me jobs. I've solved more cases than you'll see in your lifetime."

"That's because you're so cute you can talk your way into anywhere just by batting your eyes."

"Shut up. Though you're right, I have to admit."

"Of course I'm right." Dan picked up another magazine and flipped a few pages.

Susie pulled a pack of cigarettes from her suitcase and stuffed them into her jacket pocket, pulling the jacket back on. "I'm taking a walk. Who knows how far I'll have to go before I can have a stupid cigarette in peace."

"Out of character, you mean," Dan added. "You really hate these jobs where you have to act civilized, don't you?"

"Whatever." The front door of the suite slammed as she left.

CHAPTER SEVEN

Sadie dropped her bags on the bed in her room and shook her arms. It was tiring, doing this much shopping. But how could she resist? Every town offered something different and Cranberry Cove always provided a blast of a buying spree. She wasn't about to pass up the opportunity to improve her wardrobe. Besides, the more clothing the better, she always figured. It let her change her looks anytime she liked. Not that she often changed them. She was proud of the way her personality could fit into a variety of jobs without disguises. So many detectives reveled in changing their physical appearance with each assignment. They were amateurs.

Her own San Francisco boutique, Flair, reflected her true personality, not to mention it was the perfect front for her other business. She loved clothing and accessories, so she wasn't playing a role on the days she worked the counter. Her sales girls were equally enthusiastic, which was a good thing. It kept them busy in front when she needed to focus on assignments in her securely dead-bolted office behind the store.

She picked up the red sweater she'd purchased, admiring the ruffle around the neck. "Widow's wealth," she'd told that sweet little twenty-something. That was an understatement. The bank accounts, stock certificates and real estate holdings that Morris Kramer, her third husband, had left her when he kicked the bucket would last her for a good decade.

Maybe she should consider taking some jobs in Paris or Rome. She could certainly afford to. Well, there was that pesky language problem. She shouldn't have cut class for those courses when she was younger. But how was she to know she could use those languages to her advantage later on? Typical student, she'd never bought into that philosophy. Twenty-twenty hindsight, as they say. Now she knew better. Everything came in handy at some point.

She grabbed the purple skirt. Red Hat Society, right! That little Susie hadn't even known what that was. She could have spit out any excuse to mix those colors and it wouldn't have mattered. The truth was, that skirt was a great match for a lavender beaded blouse she'd picked up on a recent assignment in Seattle. She could dress it up with shiny black boots. That outfit would be perfect for an occasion when she rinsed out the red dye and sported a salt and pepper look.

She rummaged through the rest of her purchases – metallic gold slippers; every gal needed a pair of those! The turquoise and coral poncho she'd found at the co-op would be exquisite with the jewelry she'd bought in Santa Fe. Just as the fringed leather jacket would complement the boots she'd brought back from Montana. But especially enticing was the black satin lingerie set, slinky nightgown and matching robe. As much as she missed Morris, there was no harm in keeping an open mind toward the future.

Carefully, she replaced the purchases in their bags, lining them up on the cushions in the little bay window. Pulling out her knitting needles and a vibrant, purple skein of mohair yarn, she settled in beside them with her thoughts. The sitting area was a nice touch in an otherwise basic room. Not that there was anything wrong with the room. It just wasn't her particular cup of Scotch. The blue and white décor struck her as dull. Still, it fit the nature of a bed and breakfast.

One of the perks of her trade was getting to travel. She knew she'd be bored if she stayed in one place too long, though San Francisco felt as close to home as anywhere. She might have moved there on her own even if Morris hadn't had to be there for that luxury hotel project. There was a charm to San Francisco that spoke to her. She adored the majestic span of the Golden Gate Bridge, the smell of freshly baked sourdough bread at Fisherman's Wharf and the exotic atmosphere of Chinatown. It had been a no-brainer to stay after Morris died.

Other cities registered high on her favorites list, as well. Santa Fe had been a blast when she had tracked down a cheating husband for a woman in Albuquerque. She'd found a fabulous painting of chili peppers at one of the many art galleries there. It fit in with the kitchen décor of her San Francisco penthouse perfectly. Of course, Santa Fe was worth a visit just for the food. How she loved the southwestern spices!

Charleston was another favorite, though that had been a tougher assignment. Embezzlement was much harder to prove than infidelity. She was lucky to have friends in the banking industry – thank you, Morris! Those contacts were able to get inside information to her about suspicious deposits and transfers to overseas accounts. What was it she had purchased there? Ah, one of the sweet grass baskets at the market place, the largest one the craftswoman had for sale. It held the massive collection of mail order catalogs in her living room. She saw no reason to stop her shopping sprees just because she was home.

That brought her back to this assignment, which was going to be even tougher. For one thing, she already liked

Molly. That never helped. The cheating husband in Santa Fe had been an obnoxious jerk. Busting him had been rewarding. He deserved it. But Molly was genuinely likable, soft-spoken and sweet. It was hard to believe she could be involved in crime, but it wasn't her job to judge. She'd tracked her down, which was half the job finished. Now she just had to keep her own emotions out of the mix, find the evidence and get out of Cranberry Cove. Without drawing attention to herself, of course, or she'd lose one of her favorite vacation and shopping locales.

She'd hesitated to take on the assignment, truth be told. The idea of tracking a person others might also be tracking didn't sit well. Binky had made it clear he'd discussed the case with other investigators, though he said he'd given her more details. That gave her an advantage but still, didn't guarantee her a spot in the lead. She'd kept an eye on the rearview mirror while driving up to Cranberry Cove. More than once, she thought she was being followed. Each time the car behind her turned off the road. Paranoia, she told herself. It was part of the business.

A second hesitation had been the nature of Binky's story, which hadn't rung completely true. Binky had seemed a little "off" when he said he was trying to help the police solve a robbery. It wasn't like him to be on the right side of the law. He was a bizarre man, Al "Binky" Martelli. Of course, no one else called him Binky. It had started as a joke when they were first married. Although the marriage had ended, the nickname lived on. For decades they had kept up an occasional correspondence. She had agreed to take the case to help him.

Now she was having second thoughts. Nothing that Binky had described about Molly matched what she'd seen since she'd arrived in Cranberry Cove. She'd expected a tough, worldly girl, maybe with harsher features and darker clothing. Binky had sent only a vague physical description based on security camera footage.

On the other hand, the area of the assignment suited her. Binky was sure the northern coast of California was where the girl had headed, which is why he had contacted Sadie in the first place. She welcomed any excuse to drive up the coast. If someone wanted to pay her to do it, who was she to argue?

CHAPTER EIGHT

Mr. Miller set his briefcase on the bed and opened it, taking out his morning pills. He set each bottle in a neat row across the desk and opened the plastic seven-day container that he used to keep his prescriptions straight. There were so many of them, it was the only way he kept from being confused. Red pills, white pills, blue pills, striped pills. There was one for blood pressure, another to settle his stomach, another for a blood thinner and yet another for his diabetes. It was not a surprise that he'd gathered the physical maladies that he had. He'd always been sickly as a boy, missing school and normal childhood activities. His mother had put him to bed at the first sign of a sniffle or cough. Other children had teased him about being babied. But it was true that he was sick a lot.

Counting out the pills with precision, he sorted them into the daily compartments. He reprimanded himself for not doing it before. He always prepared carefully for trips, with great attention to detail. But the situation had come out of the blue and required packing in a rush. How he hated rushing around. It broke up his disciplined lifestyle. That was not a good feeling, not good at all. Things needed to be in order, like the cabinets in his kitchen, like the meticulously sorted clothing in his closet. Chaos unsettled him. A doctor had suggested OCD. Maybe therapy would help? That made no sense to Mr. Miller. Out of order was simply out of order. It was not the natural way of life, in his opinion. Lack of organization was intolerable.

He rarely got travel assignments from the insurance company he worked for. He knew they considered him odd and reclusive. They were right; he *was* odd and reclusive. They knew better than to send him out on most cases. Places like New York, Boston or Philadelphia made him nervous. Trashcans overflowed and window signs weren't always straight. He was relieved they never asked him to go to those locations. There was nothing orderly about big cities. But a tiny town, a little inn that was neat and clean – this suited him. And the assignment couldn't have been more serendipitous. He could hardly believe his luck when his supervisor handed him the case.

Cranberry Cove was bearable, Mr. Miller thought as he dropped a blood pressure pill in each plastic square. He'd been quite pleased when he arrived. Molly hadn't pushed him for conversation, and the room's décor was exactly as he liked, right down to the fishing theme. Every picture hung straight and each trinket – there were not too many, thank heavens! – was dust-free and set apart. That was one of the worst things as far as he was concerned, seeing items lumped together. How people had such poor senses of spatial arrangements baffled him to no end. This was one reason he avoided shopping malls. Those window displays! Didn't people know how to set items in straight or circular patterns? No one should be allowed to do displays without those perceptions.

He finished filling his pillbox and snapped the lids of his prescription bottles shut. He replaced them in the briefcase, each one in an elastic-banded spot. Once the bottles were lined up and secured, he pulled out his notebook, opening it carefully to avoid wrinkles or smudges. Pristine paper was all he could tolerate. Even the slightest mark could make him hyperventilate.

It was clear why the agency had assigned him the case. His observation skills were outstanding. The only directions he'd been given were to observe the innkeeper and take notes. He was instructed not to interact with her any more than necessary, which was fine with him. He didn't care for conversation. Besides, keeping to himself would surely work to his advantage this time, considering his own agenda.

He hadn't written any notes the day before, after arriving at the inn. He'd merely observed. After all, that was his assignment. At night he rarely wrote notes since it interfered with his before bed ritual, which took two hours. One full hour of exercises. Twenty stretches over one toe, twenty stretches over the other. Then twenty knee bends with arms extended to the front, parallel to the ground, followed by twenty waist twists side-to-side, always starting to the right. He repeated the sequence twenty times, then set a timer for twenty minutes of meditation, during which he mentally lined up the items he'd seen that day. Birds, flower pots, red barns or telephone poles, it didn't matter what the items were. He visualized them and set them in straight lines, in rows of twenty. After this first meditation, he brushed his teeth and said two of the prayers he'd learned as a boy. He repeated the routine, starting with the exercises, right down to a second tooth brushing and two more prayers. Then he slept.

He looked over the blank page in the composition book and pulled his fountain pen from his pocket. Inscribing the words, "Day One Observations," he proceeded to describe his first impressions of the innkeeper. She was approximately five foot five inches – how he hated this part, not being able to measure exactly – with brown hair and brown eyes. She was quiet and polite, not too pushy. What a relief that had been!

She'd worn a solid, navy blue skirt and a red cardigan sweater with sixteen buttons down the front and one wayward thread hanging from the left seam. He paused and bit his lip, thinking of the dangling thread. He blinked his eyelids twenty times to force himself to refocus.

He moved on to "Day Two Observations," detailing the breakfast she had served. She'd worn tan slacks with no cuffs, a black T-shirt and print apron with coral seashells and a rickrack trim. She'd also worn sandals. He disapproved of that, seeing as it was a culinary setting. But his personal feelings were not part of objective observations, so he noted only the tan leather and silver buckle of each sandal. He paused and then added that the salt and pepper shakers on the table had been perfectly aligned. That is until that older woman had knocked a salt shaker over. He shuddered remembering the incident.

He closed the notebook and put the fountain pen back in his pocket, then removed it, placed it on the desk and then replaced it once again in his pocket. He always felt out of sorts when away from home, when he was forced to change his habits. He tried as best he could to recreate his routine when he traveled, but it was never the same. Home felt secure. Being away from home meant being out of his comfort zone, yet what good detective always stayed home?

The head of the agency was a stickler for details. He called Mr. Miller "The Detail Man," which was a high compliment, as far as he was concerned. It was one of the things he respected about the agency, the way they valued specific information. Few people truly appreciated an orderly report. They were result oriented. Results meant getting paid. The faster the results were in, the sooner the money was in the bank. Or *back* in the bank, in this particular instance.

Personally, he didn't care about money, which was good, since the agency paid so poorly. He had accrued a hefty savings over the years and invested his money so wisely that he knew he could retire young. What he did care about was order. He hadn't missed a single Perry Mason episode while growing up and it bugged him to this day how many cases could have been solved sooner. If only Della had made orderly lists for Mr. Mason instead of just making phone calls and discussing things. Now, if he, Mr. Miller, had been on those cases, it would have been different. They never would have missed anything. The shows might have been shorter, but they could have solved more than one mystery per episode. Maybe ten or twenty – yes, twenty would have been perfect. One every three minutes…no, make that two minutes and twenty seconds, to allow for advertising.

The point was people were not as detail oriented as they needed to be, especially in the field of detective work. With this thought in mind, he opened the notebook again and looked over his current list. Double-checking everything was crucial. Had he missed anything? No. Every detail about her was recorded – clothing, hair, jewelry and behavior. One more day of observations and he would have a list to turn in.

CHAPTER NINE

Molly set the registration book aside and turned her thoughts to the following morning's breakfast. No one was checking out and no one was arriving, so she'd have the same number of mouths to feed. She'd need to make a market run that afternoon, in time to be back before the wine and cheese hour at five o'clock. This reminded her to pick up a round of Gouda cheese, as well as the breakfast supplies. As for the morning menu, French toast with fresh raspberries would make a main entrée. She'd do a basic egg scramble with herbs from the inn's garden to go along with it. And maybe...yes, fresh squeezed juice, cranberry applesauce and two types of baked goods, for variety.

List made, she set it aside and thought about the current mix of guests. They were an odd group, no two people similar in any way. The newlyweds were young and sweet. The effervescent woman from San Francisco was a bundle of enthusiasm. The quiet businessman was nondescript – obviously someone who liked to be left alone. And that other man, that...handsome, infuriating man! He was harder to figure out, but she'd put her money on the playboy type. Wealthy, spoiled, entitled...the list could go on and on. She'd worked with people like that back at the ad agency in Florida.

She shuddered as thoughts of Florida crossed her mind again. She tried hard not to think about the life she left behind, but reminders still nudged their way in. The phone was a perfect example. She never answered it directly, but she would still reach for the phone when she heard it. She was prompt about returning messages, usually getting back to people within a few minutes. Excuses were easy – "I just stepped out" or "I was helping a guest." No one ever questioned why a machine answered in this day and age. It let her screen the calls.

What made her nervous were the hang-ups in voicemail. They were probably nothing important, only computer solicitations or marketing surveys. And prospective guests would rather talk to a person than a machine, so they were likely to call back another time. Still, those blank messages reminded her of calls she received after the bank robbery – nothing but empty space on the other end of the line or, worse, the hushed sound of someone breathing. Had those come from whoever was sending her the anonymous threats? Or were they coincidental?

Maybe there wasn't really any way to leave a life behind. All a person could do was hope for the best. She doubted there was such a thing as absolute safety. But distance could help, even if only to keep paranoia from overtaking her daily life.

Just because you're paranoid doesn't mean they're not after you. Funny how she'd always found that saying humorous – until it became too real.

As for the debonair guest, maybe she was being too hard on him. It wasn't fair to associate his behavior with her former company's snooty clients. Perhaps he just came across as arrogant, but was, inside, as nondescript as Mr. Miller seemed to be.

"Excuse me."

Molly practically flew out of her chair at the sound of the deep voice. She turned around to find Bryce Winslow standing not quite three feet away, a charming grin stretching from cheek to cheek. *Personal space,* she chided, silently. *Comfort zone.* She pressed her back against the desk, trying to give herself breathing room.

"What can I do for you?" She spit the words out with less composure than she would have preferred.

Bryce smiled. "How would you like to help me?"

There's such a thing as giving too much credit where credit isn't due. Back to square one; he was arrogant, just as she'd first thought.

Tempted to throw out a smart retort, she reminded herself that he was a guest. Luckily, she also caught herself before seeing the ice bucket in his hands.

"Oh," she said. *I sound like an idiot. I LOOK like an idiot.*

"I'll be glad to fill that for you."

Another manly grin. "I can do it if you'll tell me where the ice machine is," he said.

"I'm sorry, Mr. Winslow…"

"Bryce…"

"Yes, Bryce, that's right. I'm sorry but we don't have an ice machine." Molly smiled in an attempt to appear nonchalant. "I'll fill it in the kitchen for you." She edged her way alongside the desk and headed for the kitchen. Was she imagining it or had he kept his same position, forcing her to maneuver a way out of the close space? Yes, she had him nailed correctly from the start – self-assured, used to getting his way, used to getting his women.

Molly let the kitchen door close behind her, relieved to have a moment to herself to recover from being startled.

Whether it was simply from the unexpected interruption or Bryce's presence, the effect was the same: her nerves were rattled.

She opened the freezer and filled the bucket, making a mental note to install an ice machine somewhere. Perhaps she could convert a hallway closet that was far enough from guest rooms to avoid disturbing them. The old-fashioned metal ice trays that she'd inherited from Aunt Maggie worked fine, and she kept them filled even when the larger freezer container was full. But it would be better for the guests – and her sanity – to have ice accessible to everyone.

Returning to the front of the inn, she found Bryce leaning casually against the wall next to her desk, arms crossed, one foot kicked across the other. She extended the filled ice bucket toward him and watched him pause just long enough to tease her before taking it from her hands. Whispering a dramatic "Thank you!" he grinned once more before vanishing up the stairs to his room.

CHAPTER TEN

This was not going to be easy. Bryce Winslow shut the door to his room and set the ice bucket on a side table. Fetching ice had only been a convenient excuse to browse downstairs. Luckily, he'd thought to take the container with him, in case he ran into Molly.

He hadn't expected any of this when he agreed to the job. The description he'd received of Molly was that of fugitive on the run, a hardened criminal. When he'd arrived at the inn, his first thought was that he was at the wrong B&B. But the address was right and the innkeeper's name was right. And, once he'd gotten into his room, unpacked and had a chance to go over his paperwork and photos, it was clear. This was the girl. At least she was the one Al thought was guilty. Bryce wasn't so sure.

It was rare that he had the problem he had now. Crooks were usually exactly as described. There was nothing appealing about them. The ones he tracked down were often slimy and unkempt. They radiated guilt. He never questioned bringing any of them in. After all, his job wasn't distinguishing the guilty from the innocent.

What was his job, anyway? Sometimes he wasn't quite sure. He thought of himself as a private investigator but knew that wasn't his reputation. He was known more as a bounty hunter, though he disliked that label. He wasn't required to research whether or not the person he tracked was guilty. The people who hired him, those on the right side of the law and those not, determined guilt or innocence. They chose the target, gave him instructions, and he brought the person in. In exchange for the delivery, he got paid. And paid well, he had to admit. Still, it was just money. He wasn't righting wrongs or making the world a better place. When it came down to it, his life was more or less a scavenger hunt. Take a list, locate the items, turn them in and earn rewards.

But something felt wrong this time. Sure, Molly was pretty and looked more like a Girl Scout than a thief, but that wasn't all. He'd already set aside the stirrings of attraction he'd felt when she'd greeted him the night before at check-in. This wasn't personal. He'd learned his lesson in that department.

That was one mistake he'd never make again, getting involved with a target. The glamorous, buxom blonde in Rio had almost cost him his life. She'd wined and dined him until he couldn't see straight, taking him to all the hottest nightclubs in the city. As it was, it cost him fifty grand, since she managed to slip through his fingers – literally. She left him oiled up and massaged asleep in a poolside cabana. That should have been an easy twenty-four hour turnaround. Instead he'd had to use inside Brazilian connections to get away from her henchmen, not to mention her jealous lover. Add to that the ten grand he forked out to appease the guy who'd hired him. Rio had been a bust.

This was different. Something deep down in his gut said he was on the wrong track. It might be the right town, the right address, even the right person, according to the job description. But she wasn't the one who'd taken the money.

If only this could be considered good news, but it wasn't. He was expected to bring her back with him within the week. Normally, he wouldn't be worried. There was always a local police department, if not the FBI, watching his back on these assignments. He usually handed the subjects he brought in over to the authorities who transferred them to a jail or delivered them to a courthouse. Usually. But the people involved this time were heavy handed and crossing them could be a mistake of epic proportions. Still, he'd escaped the Rio disaster, so he ought to be able to escape this.

Bryce tossed the ice in the basin and shook out the container, setting it aside to dry. Moving to the front window, he leaned against the sill and looked out across the bluff, at the ocean. He needed to think the situation through. Not taking her back would put him in danger. Taking her back would put *her* in danger. There was only one answer he could come up with. He was going to have to prove she was innocent. The question was, how?

CHAPTER ELEVEN

Susie strolled a good six blocks from the bed and breakfast, zigzagging from one street to another, until she was far enough from the inn to be out of sight. She hid behind a water tower and sat on a low bench, knees propped up in front of her, heels digging into the bench's seat. She leaned back against the wooden slats and pulled a cigarette from the package in her pocket. Lighting it, she drew in a fierce puff and exhaled slowly.

These were the worst scenarios for assignments, the ones where she had to play the nice girl the entire time – sweet, adored by all. It wasn't that she couldn't pull it off; she'd done it many times. But it bored her to tears, compared to the thrill of, say, posing as a prostitute or a drug dealer for the police department. Granted, she only got those assignments as bargains to get out of scuffles with the law. Still, those were her favorites, guaranteed to weave a little excitement into the job.

This current assignment was about as boring as they came. Take the setting, for a start: a bed and breakfast in a little cutesy town. There wasn't even a bar that stayed open past midnight. This seemed like a waste of a business opportunity to Susie. In a town this drab, what else was there to do at night? The bars might as well stay open just to give people a place to go. Hell, they could probably make some extra bucks out of the back room, taking bets or selling drugs. Too bad there wasn't such a place in Cranberry Cove. She could turn someone in for dealing and pick up some good stuff herself. At least that would up the excitement level of this trip.

Then there was the innkeeper herself. Molly hardly resembled some of the crooks she'd known over the years. Not that she cared. Tracking her down had been enough. She'd just have to keep up the goody two shoes newlywed cover until she could be sure Molly was the right girl. And until she found the money.

Which brought her to the main annoyance with this case: Dan Patterson. It wasn't that there was anything wrong with the Patterson Detective Agency. It was a reputable company, well backed financially by old family money. They always paid promptly. The cases they took on were solid, despite being boring. The only one drawback to working for them was being forced to team up with Dan Patterson.

Since Dan, the head honcho, had such a ridiculous, schoolboy crush on her, he tagged along on her assignments anytime he could. She knew he set these jobs up as excuses to force her to spend time with him. She avoided them whenever possible, but this time she'd decided to grin and bear it. The opportunity was too perfect. It served her personal agenda, provided Dan didn't catch on, which was unlikely, dimwit that he was.

Working around Molly was going to be a challenge. It would take a lot of snooping to figure out where the money from the bank robbery was hidden. Cranberry Cottage Bed and Breakfast was a decent sized establishment, compared to many small inns with only two or three rooms. The money could be in one of the guest rooms or the laundry room or the kitchen. Or the attic. There must be an attic.

Or it could be in the Cottage Suite, right under their noses. That was a possibility. At least searching there would be easy enough.

She tried to brush away the thought of Dan. The way he hovered over her and had fun playing newlyweds was creepy. She'd managed to keep him off her so far, but she'd have to start getting clever about it. His hands were wandering closer each day. During their first pseudo-married night she'd spent too much time slapping him away. In the suite, he was easy to handle. But at the inn, in front of other people, it was more challenging. As much as she would have liked to haul off and slug him at the breakfast table – just to get the day started on a clear foot, if nothing else – she couldn't. Staying in character was as important, if not more important, than physical disguises. If Molly didn't buy their cover, they'd be in trouble. Susie would be in trouble.

Susie stood, dropped the cigarette and stamped it out. She watched the grey ash blot against the cement walkway. Another butt extinguished, one of many she'd ground into the pavement over the years. Hopefully, another of many jobs done soon, as well.

CHAPTER TWELVE

Sadie had never liked handwritten notes, even when she was younger. In grade school, they were a fast ticket into detention hall. In high school, they could be intercepted and used for blackmail. In college, they paved an easy path for a student to take advantage of someone else's research. And in detective work, they were dangerous. In the wrong hands, information could be passed along to ill-chosen recipients. Enemies, maybe, or competitors.

Instead, she put her trust in technology. She had three cell phones, all registered to different names. Email addresses numbered in the dozens, many tied to websites that bore no resemblance to each other, either in business type, location or design. They were hosted by different web companies and accessed from remote servers. Thank heavens for the age of tablets, too. It used to be hard carrying three laptops with her, just to keep IP addresses separate. But the equivalent number of tablets wasn't enough to throw out her back, which is exactly what happened in Minnesota years ago. Of course, the cold air and the fact she'd walked off an airplane without stretching didn't help. But she was confident now she could sling a case full of tablets over her shoulder without pulling any muscles.

Sadie sat in the bay window of the Battenberg Room and balanced a tablet on her lap, pulling up the email of Dotty Trainor of Nebraska. Dotty was one of her favorite character disguises. She was the opposite of everything that Sadie thought herself to be. Dotty was timid, insecure, just a tad younger than Sadie – amazing what make-up could do! All in all, she was a wonderful person, one of those church-going types. She passed herself off as a florist, which allowed her to send deliveries to locations near and far – so convenient. Dotty was so self-effacing that she would never be suspected of snooping around. Sadie liked her so much that she often forgot she wasn't a real person.

There were others she was fond of, even if they were too much of a stretch to play in person. Guadalupe "Lupe" Maria Moreno was one of those. Much younger and much sexier, Sadie would have loved to live in Lupe's Acapulco villa. Even Sadie didn't have the flair that Lupe had in her closets. Closets, plural, of course, because she had five of them, each filled with ruffled skirts, slinky blouses, spandex pants, finely knit sweater dresses. There were stilettos in every color, some strappy and sassy, others simple and chic. On racks that many would use for belts, Lupe hung gold strands of semi-precious stones, sterling silver pendants and intricate beaded chokers. Four large baskets – four, mind you – were stuffed with scarves: solid, print, silk, knit, bold, sleek and everything in between. More than two hundred of them, at last count. Aside from her sensational couture collection, she drove a fire engine red Ferrari. That alone was worth envy.

Another favorite online disguise was Jane Simon, the New York jet setter. As wealthy as Lupe, her lifestyle was entirely different. Her penthouse loft looked out over Manhattan, thirty-seven stories above the pretzel vendors and newspaper hawkers. She spent more time out of the country than in, traveling to Tokyo, Paris, London and even Budapest, when she had a whimsical craving for goulash. A tall, leggy redhead, she had never been seen in person by anyone who hired her, of course. But they knew she existed online through coded photos. Each photo contained information about whatever case she was on. And she always solved them. Her batting average was perfect, as was her evasive nature.

Yes, Jane was quite a remarkable detective, Sadie had to admit. One of the best she'd ever invented.

But, enough daydreaming about her imaginary co-workers, Sadie thought. Back to Dotty. She opened a blank email to send to…Mario. Yes, Mario would do. She loved to imagine what he would be like if he were real, such a sweetheart, a kind, gentle soul, full of southern wisdom and Cuban connections. His character was handy, as well as entertaining. Binky could log into Mario's email account and read between the lines. It was their personal way of communicating.

Mario,

It has been a long time since we last talked. I hope your sister has recovered from her back surgery and that your home in Florida didn't get hit too hard during that last hurricane. You're brave to live on the gulf coast like you do, though I know you're fond of the warm water and soft sand. Of course, we get tornadoes here. Any area has its drawbacks.

I'm on a break from work and have found a charming bed and breakfast on the west coast, somewhere north of San Francisco. Speaking of geographical drawbacks, we had a small earthquake yesterday. Nothing I can't deal with, of course. But I'm certainly not in Kansas anymore!

There are some characters here, for certain. I'm quite fond of a young couple – especially the girl, who has the potential to be a great consumer. She adores shopping, though I've noticed she doesn't buy everything she tries on. She loves accessories, in particular. I'm not as fond of one guest, a traveling salesman – or something like that, who is quite eccentric. He's not my type, as you can imagine. There's another guest here, handsome and a real sweet-talker. Don't get jealous, now!

The innkeeper is a nice young woman. If she has money, she doesn't flaunt it. Or she hides it well, one or the other. I'm not sure the opinion people have of her is accurate. I'm glad I'll have a few more days to enjoy her company and get to know her better.

Say hello to your dear sister for me, Mario. I hope to see you the next time I pass through the south.

Yours,
Dotty

Sadie sent the email off to Mario's address and closed the tablet's cover. Her coded communications didn't always make sense on the surface, but that was the point. She was able to pick out the important facts later, hidden between the normal chatter – where she was, what people were nearby, the date the email was sent, etc. Sort of like tossing a piece of a jigsaw puzzle into the sea – the virtual sea, that is. The pieces would float together later.

CHAPTER THIRTEEN

Molly swept through the front door of the local market and headed for the dairy section. Setting up the cheese and cracker tray for the afternoon wine hour was one of her favorite daily activities. Choosing which cheeses to serve entertained her as much as clothes shopping might satisfy others. Gouda was a given, as it was always a hit. But variety was important, too. She added a wedge of Brie to the basket. For presentation, she picked up grapes, berries and walnut halves to cascade alongside the cheese assortment. A side of warm cranberry brie bites in flaky crust would add an elegant touch.

Days without check-ins were always easier because they offered a block of free afternoon time. Today was especially easy because there also were no checkouts. None of the current guests required new linens or towels. The newlyweds just wanted privacy, the bizarre Mr. Miller had kept a Do Not Disturb sign on his door since his arrival, and Sadie had insisted everything was perfect just the way it was. Bryce Winslow hadn't asked for anything but ice, though it seemed clear he'd ask if he needed something.

Was it a week he said he was staying? Molly wasn't sure whether to be happy or uncomfortable. The business income was always welcome, though Aunt Maggie had left her with a decent operating account at the bank. But there was no mistaking the attraction she felt towards Bryce and her instincts told her it was reciprocated. That could be trouble. She could almost imagine the normal "getting to know you" conversation sliding into the abyss. "Yes, my background, let's see…I was a quiet administrative assistant for an ad agency, then I was mistaken for a bank robber, then released by the police, but stalked and accused of stealing the money via threatening notes from strangers. How about you? Where did you grow up?" She'd follow that with a nice smile. Sure, that would work well.

This had been a dilemma since leaving Tallahassee. She was young, not quite thirty. She wasn't ready to throw in the towel on romance. She tried to tell herself it was just for the time being, that the whole mess would get straightened out. But how was that going to happen? For one thing, no one knew where she was. For another thing, there was no one she felt she could trust. She'd had a few friends in Florida, but no one she felt so connected to that she'd shared the threatening letters. She'd gone to the police, but they had no leads and eventually just told her to keep her doors locked, that they didn't think she was in danger. It was all just a sick prank that someone thought up after seeing her on the news.

That was easy for others to say. To Molly, it was hardly a prank. It was a minute-to-minute living terror, constantly watching over her shoulder and checking the locks on her doors. The police had put a protective watch on her house for a while, but stopped once they decided it wasn't necessary. She might have stayed if they had kept up regular patrolling.

It was better in Cranberry Cove. The distance from Tallahassee helped and the peaceful nature of the bed and breakfast was calming. But the fear never completely left her. She wondered if it ever would.

Molly gathered her purchases and paid at the front counter, thanking the grocery store clerk for ringing the items up. On her walk back to the inn, Molly stopped at the flower shop to pick out selections for a new table arrangement. Juggling snapdragons, carnations and groceries, she left the store and took a sharp left on the sidewalk, running directly into Bryce Winslow.

"Need help with those?"

Molly's stomach fluttered at the sound of the alluring voice. It served her right for blocking her field of vision as she walked. Bryce ignored her attempts to turn down his offers of help and took the grocery bag from her arm curling it against his chest. He let her carry the flowers.

"Thank you," Molly stammered. "I'm sorry; I wasn't watching where I was going."

"So I noticed." Bryce grinned. *Smug, as usual.*

"Are you out exploring the town?" Molly asked.

"Something like that," Bryce answered. He shifted the bag of groceries from one arm to the other and stuck his free hand in his pocket.

Why was he so vague about everything? Had she noticed it before?

"So, what brings you to Cranberry Cove?" Molly said, immediately wishing she could take the words back. It wasn't her place to question why guests were there. Sometimes they volunteered information, sometimes they didn't. But she never asked straight out. What was the matter with her?

Bryce paused before answering. At least it seemed that way to Molly. "A little business, a little relaxation," he replied, finally. "I'm a writer. It seemed like a quiet place to get some work done on a novel."

"How interesting," Molly said. "What's it about?" She glanced sideways, Bryce's face framed on one side by a purple snapdragon and the other by a white carnation.

Again Bryce paused. "Well," he said. "It's sort of an espionage plot. Guy stuff, international intrigue, government secrets, that sort of thing."

"Sounds fascinating." Molly cringed at the sound of her white lie. She'd choose a light romance or mystery any day over a spy thriller.

"I hope so," Bryce said. "We'll see when it's finished."

Molly was grateful the walk back to the inn was only a few blocks. The conversation was going nowhere and Bryce didn't seem eager to talk. She was relieved when they reached the inn, taking the opportunity to part ways in the breakfast room after Bryce set down the bag of groceries.

"Back to work," she said cheerfully, heading toward the kitchen.

"Same here," Bryce echoed, heading for the stairs. "Back to the book."

CHAPTER FOURTEEN

Bryce stood at the window in his room again, looking out at the ocean and cursing. What on earth had he done now, telling her he was writing a novel? He hadn't tried to write anything fictional since high school English. Couldn't he have come up with something better? With all the years of experience he'd had and all the creative covers he'd constructed in the past, that was all he had? Molly made him nervous in a way that was new to him. He was walking a fine line.

He shoved those worries aside. She might not even ask about the book again, and if she did, he would claim writer's block to avoid discussing it. He had a bigger problem. He had to try to prove her innocence. Could he do it without revealing to Molly why he was there?

His brow furrowed as he tried to figure out where to start. Jobs involving Al were always tricky, if not dangerous. He was going to need solid facts for Al, who wasn't likely to trust someone else's hunches. Things either made sense to him or they didn't. There was no in-between. Saying, "I just feel certain she's innocent," wouldn't get him anywhere. It could even get him a permanent concrete vacation. Which meant, in order to get everything in line, Bryce was going to have to start from the beginning. That is, looking at the information that made Al certain she was guilty.

The bank had been robbed on a Friday, which was a stupid day to try to pull that off, anyway. Fridays were busy. There were too many things that could go wrong. But that was beside the point. Or was it? That could reveal the thief as an amateur, which could be helpful information. Except that Al didn't use amateurs, so that was out.

Bryce ran the details through his head. The bank got hit shortly before noon. By that evening it was all over the news, including footage from security cameras. He'd seen the footage himself and had to agree, the outside camera made Molly look guilty. The inside cameras proved that she wasn't at the window that had been robbed. She'd been at the next one over, standing one minute and crouching down the next. That would have been when all the customers hit the floor, which made sense. That also should have proven she was innocent, but that's where it got complicated. The actual robber had also ducked below the counter before leaving. Could money have been exchanged? Were words exchanged? Was it possible they were both in on the job?

The outside cameras showed the robber leaving in one direction and Molly, in the other. The robber was running, which was suspicious. Molly was walking, which appeared less suspicious. Still, they looked almost identical – coats, hair, height, weight. Well, Molly might have a few extra pounds on her, but that could have been a difference in clothing.

Why had the robber ducked below the counter before leaving? It only took up time when she could have been on the way out. Had she told nearby customers to keep down until she was gone? Or had she stashed the money inside her coat? Or…had she passed off the money for later pick-up, in case she was caught on the way down the block? And if she handed it to Molly, all eyes would have been on the running thief while Molly strolled out of the bank and down the block in the other direction. That could have been a clever diversion.

There was a problem with that, though. If Molly had been part of the robbery team to begin with, why were they trying to track her down? Unless she had turned on them, taken the money and run. And that would be an amateur move. No professional would be dumb enough to double-cross Al like that. This was either a job pulled off by inexperienced thieves or a bungled plan.

Another possibility crossed his mind. The actual thief might have taken advantage of Molly being there to make it look like the money was taken, but had really passed it off to someone else after running, someone else that ended up keeping it, thereby double-crossing the initial thief. Ducking below the counter might have just been coincidental.

Or a more plausible theory: Molly had been set up. Bryce turned away from the window and paced. This was something that had crossed his mind before. It was an awfully big stretch to think that the robber looking so much like Molly wasn't planned – same height, hair color and length? And wearing an identical coat? Molly had run errands on a regular schedule, according to several former co-workers he had interviewed before leaving Florida. It wasn't inconceivable that the crook had staked out the bank, observed her daily routine and clothing and then set out to duplicate her appearance. Molly didn't seem the fashionista type. She would have worn the same raincoat most of the time. That would have been easy to match. As for the hair, maybe the thief wore a wig to add to the disguise? No, the thief's hair could easily have been cut and dyed to match Molly's.

His instincts told him Molly was innocent. He'd thought finding a stash of stolen money at the inn would be one way to prove her guilty, but that theory was out. The real thief must have passed it off to another person after leaving the bank, or might have stashed it somewhere along the way, intending to retrieve it later. Someone else could even have stolen it during the escape. That quick duck below the counter might have had nothing to do with the money. It could have been a threat for Molly to keep quiet. Still, he had a hunch it wasn't accidental. The thief had set Molly up to look guilty, regardless of how the rest of the event played out.

That still left the bigger question unanswered: Where was the money? If Molly was innocent, as he suspected, and the money disappeared before it reached Al, did the thief hide it or did someone else take it?

One way or another, he'd need more answers to prove Molly's innocence. And the more he mulled it over, the more it seemed clear. He was going to have to open up to Molly about why he was really in Cranberry Cove. He'd just have to hope this tactic didn't backfire.

CHAPTER FIFTEEN

Susie slipped back into the barn suite, hoping to find Dan napping. It was one of his only saving graces. Reading, television, heavy meals, you name it, put him out like a baby. His narcoleptic tendencies worked to her advantage in several ways. For one thing, she didn't have to fend off his advances all the time. For another, it gave her breaks between his needy conversations. Why didn't he get himself a real girlfriend or even a wife if he needed that much constant companionship?

But the best perk to his napping was getting the chance to snoop around on her own and use assignments to her personal advantage. For example, maybe Molly had hidden the money in the inn. She and Dan weren't responsible for recovering the exact dollar amount. Any thief could spend part and save part. Or divide a stash up into different hiding places. There was nothing to say how much Molly had hidden away, so who could say how much they would find? Susie figured a 20 percent cut alone was fair, just for putting up with Dan. If she found it on her own, she could skim her rightful share off the top and say she found the amount the thief had left over.

Dan was crashed out on the suite's sofa, a magazine draped across his chest. That left the living room off limits for exploration, but the bedroom was open game. Susie stepped into the room and closed the door silently, locking it. Even if Dan woke up and found it locked, it wouldn't seem suspicious. After all, she locked him out every night.

She looked around the bedroom. Even with her extravagant tastes, she had to admit it was nice. The four-poster bed was solid and expensive, with intricate carvings across the headboard. The bedding itself was of fine European fabric, an ensemble that encompassed the comforter, six shams, a bed skirt and a fluffy afghan throw. The scalloped window treatments and imported throw rugs all matched the color scheme.

The furniture was a little sparse for her taste, but there was only so much that would fit in a restored barn suite. She would have liked a Jacuzzi tub in the room – as long as Dan was on the opposite side of the door – but the antique furniture would be easier to search, anyway. It was bad enough she was going to have to tap each tile in the bathroom to listen for hollow spaces where someone might hide contraband.

She started with the bed itself, running her hands up and down the posters, looking for cracks or openings. There weren't any. The wood was solid. The only joints were located where the bottom panel and headboard attached. Sliding under the bed, Susie was relieved to find old-fashioned slats holding the box spring and mattress. Slat frames were always the easiest to check. She ran her fingers along each one-by-four slat of wood, determining that they were solid and flat against the box spring. There was nothing wedged in between.

The dresser was her next target. She pulled out each drawer, checking it for a false bottom and inspecting the area behind it. Finding nothing but dust, she sighed. Shouldn't the cleaning people be getting the inside of the drawers when they dusted? She made a note to herself not to unpack anything from her suitcase. She didn't need anyone's discarded dust, or germs, for that matter.

There were four paintings hanging on the walls – a large landscape of the coastline, a medium watercolor of one of the town's water towers and two long, narrow panoramas. A quick check behind all four indicated thin backings in the matting, not thick enough to hide anything. The frames themselves were narrow and solid. And there were no compartments or holes in the walls behind the pieces, which would have been too obvious, anyway. Anyone who could create a new life for herself, three thousand miles away from a crime, would do more than stash money behind framed paintings.

Susie had just finished inspecting the interior of a standing wardrobe and was contemplating whether or not to investigate a crawl space panel – how she hated spiders! A knock on the door caused her to jump.

"Getting dolled up for me in there?" Dan laughed.

"In your dreams," Susie shouted back.

He was pathetic. If his jobs didn't pay so well, she would have walked away from the Patterson Detective Agency long ago. Instead of hanging out in a measly coastal town, she could be on assignment with that hunk she worked with on the cruise ship around the Greek islands. Or Paolo, from Brazil.

"Just trying on outfits for that fancy dinner you're taking me to tonight."

"What dinner would that be?" Dan asked.

"Whichever one puts us at a prime table in the most prestigious restaurant in the area." She smiled. Might as well play it up and get a good meal out of the trip. There were always side benefits to traveling with someone who had deep pockets, even if that someone was Dan.

"In this town?" Dan said. "I doubt it. Maybe a cute café, if we're lucky. I'll treat you to some clam chowder. How does that sound?"

Susie opened the door and walked into the living area, sitting on the couch. She ignored Dan when he glanced at her legs as she crossed one over the other. "You forget what a good detective I am, my dear Mr. Patterson. I never go out on assignments without thoroughly researching an area first. That's one of the reasons you hire me, remember?"

"And what did you find?" Dan prodded.

"There is an exquisite restaurant north of here called Ocean."

"That's it, just 'Ocean'?" Dan asked. "Couldn't they think up a better name?"

Susie rolled her eyes. "You're so small town, Dan. You really need to get out on some bigger assignments. Don't you have those connections in Amsterdam that you used to have?"

"What connections in Amsterdam?" Dan said.

Oops. She tried not to get her detectives mixed up, but it happened now and then. Dan didn't need to know too much about her other, more sophisticated jobs.

"Oh, did I say Amsterdam? Sheesh, where is my mind today?" Susie laughed. "I mean Annapolis, maybe some D.C. jobs." *Close call.* "Anyway, that's where you're taking me tonight. I've got a craving for lobster and I hear they fly it in fresh."

"You couldn't have lobster the next time you're in Maine, maybe? Think of the environmental benefit of saving the transport fuel."

Susie laughed. "I didn't realize you were such an ecology-minded guy. Next thing I know, you'll be telling me to recycle. Don't hold your breath."

"I always hold my breath around you, darling."

"Am I going to have to take this crap from you the whole trip?"

"You love it." Dan laughed.

Knowing he was annoying her on purpose only aggravated Susie more. It was like flashing back to junior high school.

"Let's get one thing straight right now," Susie said. "I'm doing you a favor by coming out here to this rinky-dink town. You could have come on your own. But you asked me for help, so deal with it. When we work together, it's on *my* terms. Those are the rules – always have been, always will be. Got that?"

A sheepish smile was the only answer she got, which was what she'd aimed for. Some men just had to have the law laid down for them. For now, Dan was back where she wanted him.

CHAPTER SIXTEEN

Sadie sorted through the credit and debit cards in her wallet and headed into town for another round of shopping. This time she planned to entertain herself with a favorite game – spending money as if her characters were doing the spending. Withdrawing three hundred dollars from Jane's account at the local bank's ATM, she wandered along the town's main street, stepping into stores to browse.

Jane would have been the obvious choice for this job. She always managed to get to the bottom of things. And Binky trusted her completely, just as he trusted anyone Sadie recommended. He didn't mind Jane's constant travel and inability to connect in person, which was unusual for Binky. He was more inclined to insist on meeting anyone he hired, as well as to keep close tabs throughout a job. It saved time later, finding out in advance who could be trusted and who couldn't. He'd never met Jane and loved her, anyway.

The truth be told, most people in the business were afraid of Binky, though Sadie knew he'd never hurt her. His reputation was enough to scare most sane detectives away. But Jane was a good match for him. She feared nothing and got away with everything. She was a legend. Of course she was a legend, Sadie thought as she laughed. Occasionally she had to pat herself on the back for the creative identities she concocted. But this time, he wanted only Sadie.

Still, security demanded that Sadie erase a few of her own tracks, so Sadie put herself in a Jane frame of mind and stepped into Lil's Little Nothings. The modest negligees in the front display window didn't fool Sadie. She'd shopped there before and knew the real gems were hidden in the back of the store. Jane didn't live a conservative life. The flings she had around the globe required a steady acquisition of sexy lingerie.

Sorting through the more risqué selections, Sadie lifted a lacey thong in the air, letting it dangle from her fingers. How did people wear these things, anyway? And why were they so expensive? There was almost nothing to them. Well, they suited Jane. Sadie did a quick note of the item's details and set it back on the display.

"Looking for something for a bridal shower, maybe?" The sales girl's voice startled Sadie. In addition, she was rather insulted. Why would the girl just assume the thong was for someone else? *Really! Besides – a bridal shower? My, times had changed.*

"No, dear," Sadie said, thinking quickly. "This is for a retirement dinner! We just love to give little gag gifts at the office. But I'm going to think it over." She smiled at the sales girl's puzzled expression and moved to another rack, this time inspecting a fluffy chenille bathrobe. The coral shade was a little light for her personal taste, but the softness of the fabric made up for it. She handed it to the sales girl.

"I'll take this for now. It'll be perfect for the cool evenings you have up here on the coast." *Jane wouldn't be caught dead in this rag,* Sadie thought. She'd go for the low-cut, slinky red satin number on the mannequin next to the counter.

Sixty dollars down and two hundred forty to go, Sadie moved on to Boots 'n Belts. Ignoring the four-inch black leather thigh-highs that Jane would have preferred, she picked up flats in a leopard print. They'd be easy on the feet and fun on the accessory front, perfect for wearing back in the inn with black pants and a similar animal print blouse. She'd wear that outfit for the wine and cheese hour, maybe try to chat up that hunky guest from breakfast.

She had to admit to being impressed that he'd commented on her jogging suit. She wasn't naïve enough to think the outfit was flattering, but admired a man who knew how to dish out compliments. Some men just didn't have the knack for it. Morris hadn't. He was the kind of guy who wouldn't notice a new hairstyle for days. If he did, he wouldn't say anything. Or he might, but it would be a casual comment, probably because he knew better than to admit he hadn't noticed the change. Still, Morris had been devoted – good company and always wanting the best for her.

Sadie loved shopping in Cranberry Cove, and she had no trouble finding other items to purchase. One window displayed a fuchsia silk shawl with abstract swirls of turquoise that she fell for. Another had a double row black beaded necklace that would go with half the clothing items she owned. She returned to the inn with only fifty dollars left. Just a little something extra for the next shopping spree, she thought as she tucked the cash away in a zippered pocket on her make-up bag. It never hurt to have a little extra cash around.

Changing outfits and slipping on the new leopard-print flats, Sadie touched up her makeup and puffed up her hair. She pulled a tiny bottle of Chanel No. 5 out of her suitcase and placed a drop behind each earlobe – not too much. She never went overboard on fragrance. Too many people were sensitive. She'd seen the heads that turned in coffee shops when overly perfumed customers walked past tables. There had even been a waitress at one of her favorite haunts who had that unfortunate habit. The server was wonderful, but Sadie had to hold her breath when ordering, not something easy to do.

Freshened up, she headed to the inn's dining room and poured herself a glass of Chardonnay. She set a few crackers on a napkin and sliced some Gouda cheese to put on top of them. Picking an armchair next to an oak side table, she sat down and looked around. Molly had done a nice job decorating the place. She could see herself returning in the future, though obviously that could be a problem if the case played out the way Binky thought it would.

She wasn't certain the information she had was accurate, but everything pointed to Molly being connected to the bank robbery. The old news broadcasts from that night looked like her. Had she assumed the distance between Tallahassee and Cranberry Cove was enough to get away? Sadie had many questions and few answers.

The quiet innkeeper didn't seem the type to be involved in a bank robbery, but then again, one never knew. There were plenty of circumstances on the news that proved this. The calm, next-door neighbor ends up being a murderer, much to the horror of those who thought they knew him. The loving husband or father is found to be exactly that, but to more than one family. All those business trips had been anything but work related. Didn't anyone see it coming?

Sadie considered the possibility that Molly might have been involved with the robbery, but not of her own choosing. Perhaps she was blackmailed into participating? But that didn't make sense. In that case, the money would have reached Binky, or whoever was supposed to get it. Instead, the money was missing, making Molly appear guilty.

No, Sadie told herself, letting her initial encounters with Molly sway her would be a mistake. She needed to stay on track. Appearances could be deceiving. She couldn't let her own impression of Molly affect her objectivity. In any case, Binky didn't care about Molly. All he wanted was to get the money back.

It bothered her a little that Binky had given others information on the assignment. It was hardly necessary. Her reputation preceded her, which is why she was in high demand in the trade. She often had to turn down jobs because she had too many offers. But Cranberry Cove was a personal favorite destination. And the out-of-pocket expenses were almost nothing, a tank of gas and a few nights of lodging at a place she would welcome going to even without work. Plus the shopping – all those stores with unique items that big city stores didn't carry! These all made the assignment appealing. If she found the money, that would be a bonus, a large bonus, according to the reward details. But if she didn't it would simply be a nice weekend up the coast. She could deal with that.

The fear of disappointing Binky was the one other factor. But that was a small possibility. If she didn't find the bank stash, someone else would. Binky was all about money. He would be fine once he got his hands on it.

Sadie heard someone walking toward the dining room. She was relieved to see Bryce Winslow instead of the odd Mr. Miller. Bryce's smile was straight out of *GQ*. His casual clothing fit the bill, as well. Why hadn't Morris ever dressed like that? Or looked like that, for that matter?

Ah, Morris, Sadie thought, her mind heading off on a tangent. He'd been a good husband. Not a looker and not fond of social occasions, but a good man. As much as she loved her independent life, she missed him dearly.

"Wonderful to see you, Sadie," Bryce said. "How did your shopping excursion go? Find any good stores?"

"Oh, my, yes," Sadie exclaimed. "Cranberry Cove is one of my favorite shopping haunts! I get tired of those city stores. Besides, who wants to go out to an event and run into someone wearing the exact same thing?"

"Sounds like you come here often," Bryce said. He brought a glass of red wine over and sat down across from her, his back to the front hallway. Again, Sadie felt flattered. Rather than watching to see who else might enter, he was giving her his full attention. The man must be a pro at business functions and equally successful in the romance department, she thought. If only she were younger.

"Every chance I can," Sadie said. She sipped her Chardonnay and evaluated the possible directions the conversation might go. She was a pretty decent judge of character and Bryce seemed trustworthy.

"I live in San Francisco, so it's an easy drive up here."

"Ah, the city by the bay," Bryce said. "I dated a girl from San Francisco once. It's a wonderful city, full of culture, not to mention great bread and chocolate."

"Oh yes, the chocolate," Sadie exclaimed. "I keep a stock of Ghirardelli on hand at all times, though there's a fabulous local chocolatier next door to me, so I make sure to patronize that shop, too. You know, one must have the four food groups: wine, caviar, cheese and chocolate."

"Did I hear someone say chocolate?" Sadie recognized the sweet voice coming from the front hall as Susie's. She was wearing the new sweater from the morning's shopping trip with a soft floral print skirt and her hair pulled back in a ponytail tied with a scarf. She could have passed for a teenager, Sadie thought, though she suspected the girl was in her mid-twenties.

"You look lovely in that sweater, Susie!" Sadie said. "I knew it was a good choice for you." Sadie took another sip of Chardonnay and then set it down. "Oh dear, where are my manners," she said. "You two missed each other at breakfast this morning. Let me introduce you. Susie, this is Bryce Winslow."

Bryce stood and turned towards the front of the room, already lifting his arm for a handshake. Sadie watched Susie's face as Bryce turned around to greet her. Perhaps it was the surprise of seeing a man that handsome that caused Susie to pause. Dan was a nice guy, but he didn't have Bryce's style. This was the type of guy who could cause women to lose their breath at first sight. Which is exactly what Susie did, but it was accompanied with a split-second freeze in expression that Sadie couldn't quite decipher. Whatever it meant, it was gone in a second. Susie stepped forward and shook Bryce's hand, a sweet smile spreading across her face. Yes, Sadie thought – newlywed, but not immune to the charms of a handsome man.

"Well now, am I not a lucky man," Bryce said. "I have not one, but two lovely ladies for company." He motioned for Susie to take his seat.

"May I get you a glass of wine … Susie, is it?" Bryce posed the question to Susie with polished charm. Sadie could not see Bryce's face, but watched Susie's expression curiously as it became animated.

"Why, of course!" Susie exclaimed. "And I'd just love some appetizers, too! Maybe you could make me a little plate of whatever's there, to go with the wine." Her smile seemed to grow even wider. Clearly, she was relishing the attention and playing it to her advantage.

Bryce cleared his throat as he walked over to the table to pour the wine. "Of course," he said over his shoulder. "Red or white? The red is a Merlot and the white..." He paused to look at the label, clearing his throat again. "The white is a Chardonnay – from Napa, an excellent year."

"Chardonnay would be wonderful," Susie said, leaning back in the armchair and crossing her legs. Did Sadie imagine it, or did that same fleeting expression pass over Susie's face again?

Bryce returned with Susie's glass of wine and placed it on the side table. He set a small plate of cranberry brie bites alongside it and then stood next to Sadie, leaning an elbow on the upper corner of her chair.

"So, what brings you to Cranberry Cove, Susie?" Bryce's throat clearing was gone and the beautiful voice was back. He took another sip of wine, sauntered to the main table to refill it and returned to stand next to Sadie's chair again.

"I'm here because...." Susie paused.

My, Sadie thought, *this girl needs help*.

"She's a newlywed, Bryce," Sadie said. "Isn't that fabulous? Young love, such a wonderful thing."

Bryce laughed. "Well, yes, that is certainly wonderful. Who's the lucky man and where did you meet him?" He took another sip of wine and waited.

Susie glanced down, straightened her skirt and then looked back up.

"His name is Dan," she said, in a singsong voice. "We met...back in college. We were college sweethearts at Michigan State. You know, love at first sight and all that warm and fuzzy stuff."

Sadie watched the conversation.

"Well, you are so lucky, my dear," Bryce said. "And Dan is a lucky man. I'm afraid I haven't been nearly as fortunate in matters of the heart. My ex-girlfriends have just been…well, you know…I just haven't made the right choices."

"Is that so?" Susie said.

Sadie was growing more and more amused at the discourse between the two.

"Now, Bryce," Sadie said. "I find that hard to believe. You seem like the type that women would throw themselves at."

"Yes!" Susie said. "You certainly do!" Turning to Sadie, she added. "He probably has to fight them off."

"What do you do, Bryce?" Susie asked. "And what brings you to Cranberry Cove – surely not the wonderful shopping." She looked at Sadie and laughed.

"I'm working on a novel," Bryce said.

"Really," Susie said, either choking on her wine or hiccupping. Sadie wasn't sure which. "How exciting for you, well, for all of us, of course! Can you tell us what it's about? In detail, please." She leaned forward a bit, seemingly eager for his response.

Bryce laughed again. "Now, that would give away the surprise, don't you think?"

"Just a hint," Sadie said. "Surely you can tell us the genre."

Bryce paused, smiling first at Sadie and then at Susie. "Actually, it's a mystery. It involves international espionage, government conspiracy, that kind of thing."

"How intriguing," Sadie said. "I've never been able to follow that kind of story. But I'll certainly read yours when it comes out. How soon do you think that will be?"

"It'll be awhile," Bryce said. "I'm still doing some research. Government conspiracies are complicated, you know."

"I wouldn't know. All that top secret stuff is beyond me," Susie said, flashing another smile. "Sounds like just trying to figure out what the mystery is can be a mystery in itself."

"Yes, it's something like that." Bryce gestured towards the main table. "More wine, ladies?"

"Not for me, thanks," Sadie said.

"And none for me, either, thank you," Susie added, setting her wine glass down and standing up. "I'll save it for dinner. Dan's taking me to a fabulous place called Ocean. He's like that, always treating me to the best in life." She paused and sighed, placing one hand over her heart. "It's such a miracle, finding a man who's not afraid to make a commitment."

"As I said, a lucky man," Bryce sipped his wine without breaking eye contact with Susie.

"Oh, I'm the lucky one," Susie added, extending her hand towards Bryce. "It was nice to meet you. Maybe we'll see you at breakfast tomorrow."

"I look forward to that," Bryce said, shaking her hand firmly. A little too firmly, Sadie wondered, watching Susie pull her hand from his grasp. Waving with a beauty queen flourish, she left the room.

"You two seemed to really hit it off." Sadie smiled as she stood up. "It's a shame she's married. But don't you worry. There are plenty of girls out there just waiting to give you a run for the money."

"Ah, yes, Sadie, how right you are," Bryce said. "Some are out to do just that. Maybe even closer than you think."

CHAPTER SEVENTEEN

Susie grabbed her cigarettes and stormed out of the barn suite and around the back of the building. She'd never been so frustrated in her life. She lit up a cigarette and leaned against the back wall. Who cared if anyone saw her break character? At this point, her honeymoon was ruined – fake or not.

What the hell was *he* doing here? He didn't work these money-chasing cases. Skirt chasing, maybe, but his eyes were never on the dollar signs. And the tiny town of Cranberry Cove was a far cry from the locations he preferred. Paris, yes. Rome, yes. Small Town America? No! If he ended up in a dinky hamlet like the one he was in now, it was by mistake.

The name Bryce Winslow had a nice ring to it, anyway. She had to give him credit for that. It was one of the better names he'd used. Maybe it was even his real name. It had a touch of arrogance to it, which matched his personality perfectly. He could add a middle name to it or the initials "III" at the end. Or both, for that matter, just to spice it up.

"Well, well, what a pleasant surprise." The deep voice came from the corner of the building. Susie didn't even bother to look over. She knew the grin that would be accompanying the greeting and had no desire to see it.

"I can't say the same," she said. She extended the cigarette pack out to the side, her arm outstretched, her eyes still facing straight ahead.

"No, thanks," Bryce said. "I gave that up years ago."

In spite of herself, Susie laughed. "Right, what about in Madrid?"

"Part of the role," he said.

"Rio?"

"Tobacco field bust…"

"Moscow?"

"Too cold to not have something to do with my hands…"

"As if that was ever a problem for you," Susie laughed.

"You're still mad at me, I take it."

"Really?" Susie exclaimed. "Whatever gives you that idea?"

"Holding grudges isn't attractive on you, my dear," Bryce countered. "You should let go and enjoy the world of newlywed bliss."

"Oh, please," Susie said, "you know I'm not the marrying kind."

"No, I suppose you're not." Bryce laughed. His voice came closer. Susie shifted positions to avoid him, saying nothing.

"So tell me," Bryce continued. "Who is your current faux hubby? Please don't tell me it's that guy from St. Louis…what's his name…Dan Patterson?"

Susie remained silent.

"Ah, so I'm right on the first guess." Bryce's voice was smug. "You hate working with that little weasel. The money must be really good this time."

"It's good enough," Susie said.

"Let's see," Bryce said. "Dan Patterson works on percentage, if I recall. I bet he offered you 50 percent." He waited for Susie's response. When he didn't get one, he went on. "Oh, maybe we better make that 55 percent or even 60 percent? He's getting more desperate to spend time with you. How flattering."

"Shut up." Susie tossed down her cigarette butt and ground it out.

"Well, I hate to disappoint you, but I think this trip is going to bring you nothing but the joy of fending off Dan's advances," Bryce said. "There's no money here."

"Of course there's money here," Susie snapped. "A lot of it, too. That little mouse of an innkeeper wouldn't know how to spend good money if it accidentally fell out of her pockets onto the counter at Tiffany's. It's here, all right. And I plan to find it."

"I don't think so. My hunch is that you're on a wild goose chase," Bryce said.

Susie laughed. "And just what makes you think that?"

"Because she's innocent," Bryce said.

"You must be kidding," Susie exclaimed. "You just want me to think I'm holed up in this town suffering Dan's shenanigans for no reason. You're jealous – that's it. I'm not falling for it."

"Suit yourself." Bryce said, ignoring the personal reference. "But don't say I didn't warn you when you walk away empty handed."

"And what about you," Susie pointed out. "If this girl is innocent, you have no one to take back with you. You're wasting just as much time as I am, in that case."

"Oh, I'll find the right person eventually," Bryce said. "I just don't think this innkeeper is going to be that person."

"Well, if you're right and there's money involved, clue me in when you find out. At least that way my whole trip here won't have been in vain. Now I have to contend with both you and Dan, which is a nightmare."

"Sorry to make your life so miserable," Bryce said.

"You give yourself too much credit," Susie smirked.

"Whatever you say, Mrs. Patterson," Bryce laughed. "Enjoy your honeymoon. See you at breakfast – that is, if you lovebirds don't oversleep."

Susie rolled her eyes and trudged back to the suite, taking a wide circle of steps around Bryce, in case he had a sudden Moscow-related urge to keep his hands warm.

CHAPTER EIGHTEEN

Bryce refilled his wine glass and went up to his room, locking the door behind him. The talk with Susie had left him unsettled. Sure, they had a past. The Moscow job had been complicated, tracking down a ring of counterfeiters. With more than one person to bring in and the obvious lure of a money trail, the guy who'd hired him for that job had recommended an assistant, one in particular who had a nose for tracking money. He hadn't objected. It wasn't going to cost him anything and would probably lead him to finding the people involved in the ring sooner.

Susie, under the name Sonja at that time, had arrived on a train from Romania. Even without the red hat and scarf that served as a recognition code, he would have noticed her. A brunette at the time – he wasn't sure how he felt about the current blonde rendition – Sonja would have stood out in any crowd. She was a waif of a girl at first sight, light and fragile. It should have been his first clue that she was a pro at disguises, but what did he know at that time? He was blinded. A beautiful young woman had just stepped off a train from Romania, that was all he knew. And she was his for the duration of the assignment.

It had been cold, the January air bone chilling. Moscow was beautiful in the winter, but not as stunning as Sonja. The ice outside disappeared whenever they were inside the hotel. Of course, the plush suite, lush carpeting and satin sheets all helped. He hated to imagine how many bottles of champagne and brandy they went through during that job.

That was before he figured out that their motives in the case were different. For Bryce, it had always been about justice, bringing the guilty party in. Never vindictive, he simply believed people needed to be held responsible for their actions, whether legal or ethical. On that particular job, the counterfeiters all deserved to be caught. That was the reason he was there.

Sonja had other intentions, though it took him a few weeks to wise up. Looking back, he could see that each time he started to get close to figuring out her game, she maneuvered him in another direction. It might have been a complicated tip that she had on the whereabouts of one of the ring members or something as simple as a lace negligee. But she managed to distract him any way she could.

By the time he realized she was after the ring's money, real or not, he was already under her spell. It took a major confrontation over the ethics they both lived by before the truth hit him. She chased money, not criminals. She was a gold-digger of the detective variety. He was a smart man. He backed away quickly.

Sonja's reaction had not been pleasant. She accused him of lying and using her. How could he have resisted, anyway? She was good at what she did, a true chameleon. It was a shame they weren't on the same side. Meanwhile, he suffered through the rest of the assignment under her overbearing, spiteful guard. He had suspected she didn't get over it then. Now he knew for certain.

This posed a problem; they had opposite goals. He wanted to find evidence of Molly's innocence, and Susie wanted her guilty, simply for the sake of finding the money. Susie wasn't going to be any help this time, and she might even block his success. If he were a different man, she might have proved a distraction, especially with their history from Moscow. But he wasn't. The fling with her had been one thing when he thought she had admirable motives. However, when he realized she'd been deceitful, he lost his trust in her. Lack of trust destroyed relationships. And, in the detective arena, it wasn't just dangerous; it could be deadly. And here she was in Cranberry Cove. He was certain she was not to be trusted.

CHAPTER NINETEEN

Sadie put on a new layer of lipstick and blotted it with a tissue. She leaned in toward the dresser mirror in her room to inspect the final look. Approving, she put on a jacket and walked the few blocks to Eleanor's for something to eat.

What an odd interaction she had witnessed between Susie and Bryce. Was this how the younger generations greeted each other now? Why, in her day, people would be on their best behavior during introductions, not fall into repartee as if they'd known each other forever. There were guidelines, whether spoken or unspoken, as to how introductions should be given and received. Those dictated politeness, especially when meeting in front of other people. Susie and Bryce had been polite to each other, but the whole conversation had seemed tense. It didn't make sense.

Unless...no, that made even less sense. How could they possibly have known each other before? And, an even better question: If so, why would they have tried to hide it?

Sadie stepped into Eleanor's and looked around. It was crowded, but she saw an open table in the corner. She crossed the room and grabbed it immediately.

Sadie smiled at the young server who approached. She was soft spoken and dressed in a casual style that fit the northern coastal area. Her earrings, made of polished driftwood and beads, swayed as she handed Sadie a menu.

"Dinner for one?"

"Yes," Sadie said. "One it is."

"Everything on the menu is good. Our soup of the day is cranberry wild rice, which is served with cranberry cornbread and honey butter. There's also a special entrée tonight: Fettuccine with sun-dried tomatoes, spinach and pine nuts in a pesto sauce."

"You're just making it harder to choose, you know," Sadie said.

"How about a glass of wine to get started?"

A busser passed by, filling a water glass and removing a second place setting on the opposite side of the table.

"Thanks, but no. I just had wine back at the inn where I'm staying this weekend," Sadie said. "I'll stick with water and then have coffee after dinner. Or maybe cappuccino – we'll see."

"We have so many wonderful inns in this town," the server replied. "Where are you staying?"

"You're right, Cranberry Cove has so many fabulous places. I try to stay at different inns when I come here. This time I'm at Cranberry Cottage Bed and Breakfast. It's delightful."

"The one that changed ownership recently. The last owner passed away, used to come here a lot. We miss her," the server said. "I haven't gotten to know the new owner well. She's been here a few times, but keeps to herself. Quiet type, I figure."

"Yes, she seems to be." *I imagine she would be*, Sadie thought to herself. "By the way, is Eleanor here tonight? I'd love to say hi to her."

"Yes, she's in the kitchen. I'll send her out. And I'll give you a few minutes to look over the menu."

"No, that's fine," Sadie said before the server could turn away. "I'll have the pasta special. It sounds delicious and I've been good about carbs on this trip." *Aside from the brie bites at the inn. And the scones that morning. And a few cranberry white chocolate bars she'd downed the night before....*

"Good choice," the server said, taking the menu and heading to the kitchen to place the order.

Sadie looked around the room as she sipped her water. The décor was more artsy than representative of the ocean, which was refreshing. Light coral walls blended well with watercolor paintings of gardens and cottages. Eleanor's could have fit in anywhere. Santa Fe, for example, had many similar cafés. Larger cities like New York or Seattle did, as well. Often they were found in the hipper sections of town. College students and young professionals frequented them for their combination of good food and casual atmosphere. Sadie found this ambiance comfortable and sought out such places on every trip.

A basket landed on the table. Sadie tore a partially sliced piece of olive bread from a baguette style roll. Taking a bite, she returned to mulling over her thoughts about Susie and Bryce.

Was she imagining a connection? After all, Susie was newly married. Surely she hadn't been flirting with Bryce. Now, Bryce flirting was another matter altogether. Men like that – handsome, self-assured – invariably flirted when an attractive lady was around. But it seemed out of place for Susie. Maybe Sadie was being too judgmental, but her instincts were usually right. That conversation had been strange. On the surface, Bryce and Susie appeared to be meeting for the first time, but the undercurrent whispered familiarity.

What was it Bryce said he did? He was working on a novel. Odd that he hadn't mentioned that when Sadie first met him, though no one had asked what he did. Not until Susie did.

Susie had definitely seemed … rattled? Her behavior around Bryce was entirely different from when they'd shopped together. It was as if … yes, that was it. Bryce had been happy, though a little surprised, to meet Susie. But Susie had not been happy to meet Bryce. The tension had been apparent in her over-the-top enthusiasm.

"Why, if it isn't Sadie from San Francisco!" Eleanor broke Sadie's train of thought. "How have you been?" Eleanor dropped down into the seat across from Sadie, her thin, strong frame filling only a portion of the chair.

"Eleanor, good to see you," Sadie said. "Your place is as busy as ever – not surprising, with food this good. How you manage to keep that youthful figure of yours is beyond me."

"I don't let myself sample my own dessert menu." Eleanor laughed. "Though I did taste test a cranberry cobbler last night."

"And you're still running, I'll bet," Sadie added, shaking her head in awe. "I don't know how you do it."

"Five miles every morning. As soon as Casey heads to the hardware store, I hit the trails down by the bluff. Clears my head and gets me ready for the work day."

Sadie studied Eleanor's gray French braid and makeup-free face with envy. In her next life, she would ask for a high metabolism and natural beauty. And a good old down-to-earth husband like Casey, too. Between Eleanor's restaurant and Casey's store, the couple had created a good life.

"You didn't answer my question," Eleanor prodded. "How've you been? Last I knew you were headed off to some small town on one of your explorations."

Sadie smiled. She always gave Eleanor enough details to keep her entertained, but not enough to divulge the real purpose for her trips.

"Well, you know I love to travel," Sadie laughed. "San Francisco starts to stifle me if I never get away."

"I can imagine," Eleanor said. "You wouldn't find me living in a big city, especially one with steep hills and narrow streets. Cranberry Cove is my speed." She paused as a server set a glass of water down in front of her. "And how's your boutique doing?"

"Busy," Sadie said. "We always have customers looking for a trinket or two – either for gifts or treats for themselves if they have some extra money to spend."

"Where are you staying this time?" Eleanor asked.

"Cranberry Cottage Bed and Breakfast," Sadie replied. "The former owner's niece is now running the place, doing a good job, too."

Eleanor nodded. "Yes, Molly. I've met her a few times. I miss Maggie, but Molly seems to be stepping up to the task. I'm sure it's a big change for her after living in Florida. Isn't that where she's from?"

"Yes, Tallahassee," Sadie said.

"Well, she fits right in Cranberry Cove. Quiet, but smiles at anyone she meets in town." Eleanor twisted her head to survey the restaurant. Convinced all customers were being cared for, she turned back to Sadie.

"Any other guests there this week?"

"Just a few. An odd little businessman who keeps to himself and a handsome novelist who seems to have eyes for Molly," Sadie laughed. "Oh, and that newlywed couple. They had dinner here yesterday. They recommended the stuffed mushrooms highly. I simply must try them before I leave."

Eleanor looked puzzled. "Newlyweds? I haven't seen anyone like that in here lately. And I was here last night. Even waited on a few tables myself. We were shorthanded."

"Young, twenty-somethings? Pretty, blonde girl and a man about her age, maybe a few years older?"

"Oh, those two?" Eleanor said. "I wouldn't have guessed they were newlyweds. Hate to see a marriage start off with that much whispered bickering. I figured them for brother and sister, maybe. Or tourists who'd been traveling together too long,"

Sadie paused, mulling over Eleanor's description of Susie and Dan. It only confirmed her suspicions that something was off.

Seeing a line building up by the front door, Eleanor excused herself to help seat arriving customers. Sadie took another sip of water and ran the whole encounter between Susie and Bryce over in her mind again. What was the link that she wasn't seeing? If they knew each other, why not say so in front of Sadie? Was it that they didn't want Susie's new husband to know about a past affair? Or was it something more?

As the server slid the plate of steaming pasta in front of Sadie, it clicked. The idea that Binky might put other people on the same case came floating back to her. No, that couldn't be right, could it? Had more than one detective keyed in on Molly at the same time? Wait, make that three, considering that Bryce and Susie hadn't arrived together and clearly hadn't expected to see each other.

Sadie caught the server as she turned away from the table, calling her back.

"I think I'll have a glass of wine after all."

CHAPTER TWENTY

Molly gathered the used wine glasses from the dining room and took them to the kitchen. She rinsed them out, placed them in the dishwasher and tossed the paper napkins in the trash. Returning to the dining room, she picked up the cheese and cracker tray and both bottles of wine. Two wine glasses had not been touched. From the kitchen, she'd heard Sadie, Bryce and Susie talking. Mr. Miller and Dan must have skipped the wine and appetizer hour. Nothing strange about that, Molly thought. Not everyone is social.

She wasn't an extrovert herself, a trait that had made her one of the "out" crowd while growing up. It wasn't that she didn't have ambitions. She was just happier when life was simple. High school cliques were complicated. So were college sororities and club activities. High-level corporate work was even worse, hence her satisfaction with the administrative assistant job she'd had. But being accused of bank robbery? Complicated didn't even come close to describing it.

Sometimes she wondered if she should have stayed in Tallahassee and fought it out. Pushed the police harder, maybe, though they seemed to stop taking her calls seriously. She'd looked into hiring a private investigator to prove her innocence but found even just the retainer too expensive for her modest savings. These actions wouldn't have stopped the persistent threats. If the people who had sent the coded notes were trying to scare her, it had worked. They knew where she lived, where she worked and what kind of car she drove. Sure, she could have attempted her own investigation, but where would she have started? She had no investigative experience. And what would have kept her safe in the meantime?

Molly leaned forward, resting her forearms against the sink's tile edge. Some days she felt like a coward. Other days she felt she'd made a smart decision. Moving to Cranberry Cove and taking over Aunt Maggie's business gave her the power to start over, to create a new life.

She jumped at a light knock behind her. Spinning around, she found Bryce standing in the doorway, watching her. Had he been there awhile? Or had he entered just as he knocked?

"I was hoping to find you here," he said. His expression was relaxed, not smug or flirtatious. There was something different about him – a lack of arrogance, perhaps? It must be the novel, Molly thought. He's stuck on a section and it brought out a bit of humility. Good.

"I was just cleaning up from the wine hour," Molly said, turning toward the sink. She could feel his eyes on the back of her neck. A shimmer of heat ran up her spine.

Remembering her manners, she glanced over her shoulder. He was a guest, after all. Turning her back on him wasn't polite, even if he had interrupted her in the inn's private space.

"Help yourself to a glass." She nodded in the direction of the wine bottles and unused glasses.

"Only if you'll join me," Bryce said. Ah, Molly thought, so much for the humble moment. He knew his way around women. And he wasn't checking out for another six days or so? This wasn't going to be easy.

"I'm fine, thank you," Molly said. "But you go ahead." She bagged the cheese and crackers, putting them away before turning toward Bryce. When she did, he was holding two glasses of wine, one stretched out to her.

"Really, I shouldn't," Molly said, hesitating, but tempted.

Bryce smiled, continuing to hold the glass out. "No, I think you should. I'd like to talk to you and you're probably going to need the wine."

"Writer's block?" Molly asked. He must really be stuck. She took the glass and started for the door to the dining room.

Bryce shook his head. "No, not in the front room. Let's sit back there." His glance fell on a small kitchen table against the far wall.

Molly laughed. "Isn't the dining room a nicer place to sit and talk literature than my battered, old kitchen table, surrounded by pots and pans?"

"For this conversation, I'll be more comfortable in here, and I think you will, too," Bryce said.

Molly sighed. Did he really think talking about a novel in progress was going to ruin the other guests' reading experiences? What an ego! The book might be terrible. Still, he was determined to talk and she was too tired to argue. She sat down at the small table.

Bryce sat across from her. He swirled the wine in his glass before taking a sip and setting it on the table. He looked down, his eyes focused on the wine. Molly watched him, curious about his unusual behavior. A tingle of uncertainly ran through her. Maybe sitting in the far corner of the kitchen hadn't been a good idea.

Bryce looked up and met Molly's gaze. "I need to tell you something," he said.

Expecting him to continue, Molly watched him lift his wine to his lips, emptying the glass. He stood, walked across the kitchen, brought the bottle of wine to the table. He offered Molly more, which she declined, and then filled his own glass.

This must be one heck of a case of writer's block, Molly thought. What could she possibly offer? She didn't even know what the story was about. Some help she'd be.

"You're not going to like this," Bryce began. "But I need you to hear me out."

For the first time since meeting the handsome guest, Molly felt nervous for reasons other than attraction. This was starting to sound personal. Whatever it was, it wasn't about his novel. Instinctively, Molly pulled her arms in closer to her body.

"I'm not sure I like where this is going," Molly said.

"You'll like it even less when I tell you what I have to say, but I need you to promise to hear me out." He reached across the table with one hand. Molly wrapped her arms around her waist. What a fine line there is between danger and safety, she thought. He could be a mass murderer or an escaped convict. San Quentin was only a few hours away, now that she thought about it.

"I'm not here to work on a novel," Bryce said.

"I'm starting to get that feeling," Molly said. If she weren't so scared, she would think the situation comical. Here she was, trapped in the kitchen having a glass of wine with a guest who was about to confess to being a serial killer. Or he could be.... Molly suddenly felt sick to her stomach.

"There's no easy way to put this, so I'm just going to spit it out," Bryce said. "I was hired to take you back to Tallahassee to resolve the issue of the bank robbery."

"No!" Molly bolted from her chair. Both wine glasses flew off the table and shattered against the tile floor. She lunged for the kitchen door, but Bryce was too fast. He grabbed her and turned her toward him, holding her arms firmly. Molly struggled to pull away, but he was too strong.

"Molly, you have to listen to me," Bryce said. "I told you that you had to hear me out."

"You lied to me," Molly shouted.

Bryce released one arm and put his hand over her mouth. Her eyes grew wide with fear.

"Lower your voice," he whispered. "I'm not going to hurt you. And I'm not taking you back to Tallahassee."

Molly felt dizzy. Nothing he was saying made any sense. How did he find her? How was he involved with this, to begin with?

"I don't trust you," she mumbled, his hand still covering her mouth.

"I don't blame you," Bryce said.

It was true, Molly thought, what people say about your life flashing before your eyes just before you die. At that moment, she envisioned her childhood house, secure and safe, followed by university days when walking to her dorm room at night felt disconcerting. After that, one uneventful work errand after another, leading up to the one that turned her life upside down. Wrong place, wrong time – one routine bank deposit had sent her life into a spiral of fear.

"If you promise not to shout, I can remove my hand and explain." Bryce said. "I'm going to help you."

Right, Molly thought. If she hadn't been so terrified, she would have laughed. Holding someone hostage in a kitchen wasn't her idea of help.

Molly nodded. She wasn't strong enough to pull away, and there was no harm in hearing what he had to say.

Obviously he was going to feed her some kind of fake story, then take her back to Tallahassee. Or kill her. Or do both. Maybe if she went along with his plans, she'd have a chance to get away later.

Bryce removed his hand slowly, watching to see if she'd cry out again. When she didn't, he led her back to the table, stepping around the broken glass, and lowered her back into her chair, his grasp now gentle. He let go but didn't move away.

"Just listen."

"Sure, why not," Molly's fear began sliding into resignation. Besides, being held hostage was turning out to be exhausting. She needed to save her strength for escape. "Sit down. Obviously you're not going to let me go anywhere."

Molly ran through the current guest list in her mind, wondering if someone in the inn would hear her if she screamed. Sadie was almost certainly out looking for a new dining spot and that weird Mr. Miller hadn't come out of his room since he checked in, other than once for breakfast. The barn suite was too far away for Susie and Dan to hear anything. Calling out for help was futile.

Bryce moved back to his side of the table and sat. He kept a close eye on both Molly and the kitchen door.

"It's true that I came here to take you back to Tallahassee."

"Yeah, I got that much." Molly's voice was dull and sarcastic. "But you said you're not taking me."

"That's right," Bryce said.

"So, this is where I'm supposed to ask why not," Molly said. "Except I'm not going to believe anything you say. I don't even know who you are, other than someone who tracked me down somehow, came here and pretended to be someone you're not then trapped me in my own kitchen!

Why should I believe you?" Molly's voice rose with each statement.

"Molly, calm down." Bryce's expression was sympathetic, out of character with the smug façade he'd presented when they first met. Despite her misgivings, she felt calmer. "Just let me explain."

"I'm waiting," Molly said.

"I did come here to take you back to Tallahassee."

"You already said that."

"Yes, you're right," Bryce said. "It's nothing personal. It's what I do, bring people in."

"Bring people in?" Molly said, her voice rising again. "As in, you're a bounty hunter? You're a freaking bounty hunter?"

Bryce smiled. "I really wish you wouldn't put it that way. It sounds so Hollywood-ish. Besides, that's not exactly what I do. I work with law enforcement. Really, it's just a job."

"Just a job," Molly repeated. "Well, you found me. Congratulations. You can take me in now." She slumped back in her chair.

Bryce smiled. "You're not listening to me."

"Well, excuse me if my listening skills aren't working perfectly. I get a little stressed when being held against my will."

Bryce threw his hands up in the air. "You know what, you're perfectly free to go. Go anywhere you want. I don't think you understand what I'm saying. I'm on your side, get it?"

"Why?" Molly asked.

Bryce sighed. "Because I have good instincts. I have to in order to survive in this business. And my instincts tell me you didn't have anything to do with that robbery."

"How about this, then," Molly said. "Since you're not *taking me in*, why don't you leave and forget you ever came here?"

"No. Not without proving you're innocent."

"Shouldn't that be easy, considering I *am* innocent?" Molly could hear the exasperation in her own voice. "I don't even understand how this whole mess happened. All I did was run an errand that I'd run hundreds of times. Suddenly my whole life turned upside down, my face was on the news, threats arrived in the mail.... Do you have any idea what this has been like? Have you ever been under this kind of stress?"

Bryce thought it best not to mention the time in Italy when a fugitive tied him to the end of a gondola at night and dragged him through the canals of Venice.

Molly pressed her hands against the edge of the table and took a deep breath. Bryce reached across and slid his hands over Molly's. She surprised herself by not pulling away. His warm palms on the back of her hands were comforting. She was starting to believe his intentions were good.

"Why are you so sure I'm innocent?"

Bryce squeezed her hands, released them and laughed. "Don't take this the wrong way, OK? But I just don't think you have it in you to have pulled off what this person or people did."

Was this a compliment or an insult? Was he saying she wasn't smart enough to be a criminal?

"You're going to have to trust me," Bryce said. "You have nothing to lose."

"Are you kidding? I have everything to lose. I have a new life here, one I love."

Molly paused at the last statement. It was true. She *did* enjoy running Aunt Maggie's bed and breakfast. It suited her more than her office job in Florida had.

"I feel safe here," Molly added. "If you really think I'm innocent, why not just drop it."

Bryce shook his head. "I don't think you *are* safe."

"The police dropped it," Molly pointed out. "That should be enough."

"Yes, it should be." Bryce ran his hand through his hair. "But this has nothing to do with who stole the money from the bank. This is about who stole the money from the crooks."

"The police never said anything about that."

"Of course not," Bryce laughed. "The mastermind of a robbery isn't going to file a missing money report. The police don't know the money never made it to the ring leader."

"How would *you* know that? I thought you were working with the police?"

"I *am* working with the police. Mostly."

Molly felt a surge of manic laughter escape. "Ah, I'm starting to see a bigger picture here! I'm going to start calling you Bryce from Vice."

Bryce frowned. "I really don't think that's a good idea."

"I was just kidding," Molly said. "But whoever these people are, why aren't they going after the person who took the money?"

"You're not going to like the answer to that," Bryce said.

"Try me," Molly said.

"They think you took it."

"What?" Molly smacked her hands flat against the table's surface. "Why on earth would they? The security cameras showed the thief running one way while I walked in the opposite direction. It was all over the news. There's no way they didn't see the coverage."

Bryce opened his mouth to speak, but Molly cut him off.

"And another thing," she continued. "They would have seen that I was arrested and then cleared. That was all over the news, too."

Molly paused, thinking over the notes that had arrived after the robbery. *"We know you have it." "We will find it."* There were others, as well.

"That's what the notes were about, then," Molly said, her eyes growing wide. "They weren't pranks, were they? The bank robbers really *do* think I have the money!"

"Exactly what I've been trying to tell you." Bryce said. "And they won't stop searching until they find it."

Molly dropped her head into her hands. "So now what?"

Bryce smiled.

"Now we figure out what really happened that day."

CHAPTER TWENTY-ONE

Mr. Miller opened his notebook and looked over his observations. He couldn't shake the feeling that he'd left out something. It drove him crazy, the nagging sensation that he hadn't completed a task. It didn't matter what it was. It could be a grocery list or a dry cleaner's ticket, a crossword puzzle or a driving test at the DMV. Once the idea settled in that he'd left something incomplete, he felt distraught.

That was exactly the way he felt about his observation of Molly that morning: "Tan slacks with no cuffs, a black T-shirt and print apron with coral seashells and a rickrack trim." It just wasn't right, yet he couldn't put his finger on what was wrong. His fear, however, was that the T-shirt had been a dark navy, rather than black. It would seem a minor detail to most people, but it represented a nightmare for Mr. Miller. If he was losing the ability to detect colors correctly, what good were his observations?

His father had been color-blind and it was something he'd feared all of his life. Was it hereditary? The thought horrified him. He took pride in the accuracy of the notes he took. Color was not a detail to be taken lightly. A description of a person's apparel without mention of color meant nothing.

He stared at his notes again. The apron had been decorated with coral seashells. Which would be a better match for that – black or blue? Just that thought brought on another, even more disturbing. Could she have been wearing a black shirt with a navy trim? Or was she wearing a navy shirt with a black trim?

If he were a man prone to swearing, he would be cursing the fact that he'd skipped the wine hour. Not that he ever attended those. For one thing, he didn't drink. Alcohol weakened observation skills, and he needed to keep his skills sharp at all times. In addition, he simply didn't like to socialize. Small talk bored him and that was all he ever heard at those gatherings. Even worse, people were so general in their conversations. He couldn't get an accurate visual image with statements such as, "Her aunt likes bright colors and wears hats," or, "We just traded in our car for a mini-van." This type of conversation drove him to hyperventilate. Did they trade up from two cup holders to four, or maybe six? And did the aunt like shocking pink, form-fitting button-down cardigan cashmere sweaters or a blousy muumuu with a hibiscus print in teal and deep purple?

He closed the notebook and set it on the edge of his desk, lining up the sides perpendicular to the desk's corner. He stood back to inspect the alignment, adjusted it slightly and went downstairs. With some luck, Molly would still be cleaning up and would be wearing the same shirt.

The dining room was empty, guests already gone and wine glasses put away. A few cracker morsels remained on a side table between two armchairs. How he hated crumbs! He hesitated, looking at the table, torn between clearing off the crumbs and having to touch them. Doing so would mean returning to his room to wash his hands, which would take time. There were no cocktail napkins around to use for cleaning up, either. As much as it pained him, he turned away from the crumbs and left them.

Molly's desk alcove was also empty, which caused his spirits to plummet even further. He'd hoped, if he missed her in the dining room, to find her reviewing guest arrivals for the following day. Surely she'd still be wearing the clothing from earlier. It didn't matter. She wasn't there.

A last idea struck him as he turned to go back upstairs. It was not out of the question that Molly would prepare breakfast items after clearing the wine hour paraphernalia. She did seem like the organized sort, not that he noted personality traits. He only gathered physical descriptions. Which brought him right back to the question of T-shirt color, it was crucial that he correct his morning notes.

He crossed the dining room and leaned his ear toward the kitchen. It was difficult to hear clearly, as he didn't want his skin to touch the door, but he heard voices inside – soft, hushed voices. Two voices, as a matter of fact – one male and one female. Molly and…a boyfriend, husband or brother?

This posed a problem. He assumed the female voice belonged to Molly. If she had been alone, he might have been able to wander in as if he were lost. She could direct him back to the front of the inn. During that process, he'd get a chance to confirm the color of her shirt. But with a second voice, especially that of a man, he wasn't sure he could pull the same maneuver off.

Perhaps he could knock? He could ask for…shampoo or extra towels. Yes, that would work. Deciding the idea seemed viable, he lifted his arm to tap on the door, but stopped as the conversation became animated.

"No!" He heard the female voice cry out. This was followed by the sound of breaking glass and hushed pleading from the other person. The exchange continued, most of it too difficult to make out. At some point the phrase, "You lied to me!" came from the woman, followed by the deeper voice offering to explain. Explain what? It didn't matter. Surely it was one of the silly quarrels that couples had from time to time. All that mattered to him was finding a way to see if Molly was wearing the same T-shirt from the morning.

He edged closer, hoping to see through the crack of the doorframe. Lights below the door flickered, shadows forming as footsteps moved inside, but there wasn't enough of an opening to see around the door. He knew he'd be in trouble if they walked into the dining room. What excuse could he possibly have for listening? He wasn't trying to eavesdrop, just to confirm the color of T-shirt he had seen that morning. But that wouldn't go over well as an excuse.

He weighed his options. He could return to his room and leave his notes the way he'd written them earlier. A black T-shirt – that was what she was wearing. But how would he sleep that night? These were the things that kept him awake, details that weren't clearly defined. He really shouldn't go over notes at all. First impressions are said to be the best, just as first guesses on a multiple question quiz are usually right. But when his mind started to doubt details, it wouldn't give up until the matter was settled.

Nudging his shoulder against the door, he moved it slowly, praying it wouldn't creak. He was grateful that it was silent as he pushed it open enough to glimpse inside.

The kitchen lighting was bright, making it easy to see. Molly was indeed wearing a black T-shirt, not navy. Perfect. He wouldn't even have to adjust his notes. He could return to his room and get a good night's sleep.

He turned to leave, but paused as he overheard the word "Tallahassee." His intention was merely to take down details of what he saw, not what he heard. Still, it struck him as an odd coincidence that the conversation between Molly and the other guest mentioned that particular city. Why would she be discussing Tallahassee with someone? Wasn't she in hiding?

It didn't matter. It had no bearing on his notes. Satisfied that he'd acquired the information he needed regarding Molly's clothing, he retired to his room.

CHAPTER TWENTY-TWO

Bryce flagged down a server for coffee refills. He watched Molly as the fresh brew spilled into the cups. She still didn't trust him; he could see it in her eyes.

The corner booth of the run-down coffee shop had been the safest place to talk and grab a bite to eat. It was on the edge of town, out of the mainstream of activity, not a place other guests would go. Bryce had made sure of that, knowing that Susie – or whatever her name was this time – was around.

"Molly, you need to tell me everything you remember," Bryce said. "Any detail you can think of, even if it seems unimportant. Start by telling me if there was anything different about your usual morning routine the day of the robbery."

Molly sighed. She pushed aside a partially eaten salad and pulled the coffee cup closer.

"I was the first one in the office each morning," Molly said. "I turned on lights, made coffee, and checked the fax machines and incoming mail slot. I set up an agenda for each ad exec, with appointment times and conference calls. I stayed at my desk during the morning, handling phone calls and correspondence. I'd make sure the conference room was prepared for any business meetings – audio-visual equipment, white boards, notepads, pens and refreshments. The ad execs would wander in a couple of hours later. They kept much later hours – entertaining new clients with dinners, etc."

Molly added a packet of sugar to her coffee and stirred it.

"Who prepared the bank deposits?" Bryce continued.

"One of our main execs filled out the deposit slips and noted the amount in the online bank register. I often handled the checks, because I sorted the mail and recorded payments on clients' files. I would stamp the backs of the checks with the firm's endorsement and gather them together, paper clip them and then let the exec finish the deposit. He'd hand it back to me after he was done."

"Do you think there's a chance he was in on it?" Bryce asked.

"No, that wouldn't make sense," Molly said. "He'd been a partner in the firm for years and made good money. Why would he risk throwing his career away? Besides, he always treated me like a daughter. He wouldn't set me up for something like that."

"Not even for all that publicity on the news channels?" Bryce suggested.

"Of course not!" Molly said, exasperated. "Really, do you have to play out every angle like this?"

"Actually, I do," Bryce said. "If I want to get to the bottom of things, I have to look at every possibility."

"Fine." Molly motioned for Bryce to go on.

"OK, let's forget about the ad exec for now. What time did you leave to run errands?" Bryce leaned back in the booth and lifted the coffee to his lips, keeping his eyes on Molly.

"Around 11:30," Molly said. "Once all the routine office tasks were handled. I'd combine errands and lunch. I'd pick up something to eat back at my desk, so I could be there to answer phones while the execs went to lunch meetings."

"Did you always run your errands in the same order?" Bryce said.

"Yes."

"Which would put you at the bank at approximately what time?"

"I'd say around 11:45," Molly said. "I didn't like to carry the deposits around. It worked well because I missed most of the noon lunch rush."

Molly paused, took a sip of coffee and sighed. "Hundreds of people come and go from that bank daily. How did I end up in the middle of this?"

"Well, I have a theory about that," Bryce said. "How often do you change jackets? Or shoes?"

"Not often." Molly shrugged her shoulders. "I admit to being a creature of habit. Why change when you have a favorite jacket and comfortable pair of work shoes?"

"Well, for one thing, so a bank robber can't mimic what you're going to wear," Bryce said. "I don't think it was a coincidence that you were there when the robbery took place. I think you were set up."

"That's ridiculous," Molly said.

"Maybe so, but I think that's what happened. They used you as a decoy. One minute of confusion is enough for someone to get away from the scene. Three days of confusion on news stations are enough for someone to be on the other side of the planet."

Bryce set his coffee mug down. "Is there anything that stands out as being different on the day of the robbery?"

Molly paused, thinking. "Well, it was a little busier than usual, because it was Friday. Some people take early lunches, others get paid on Fridays and cash their paychecks. I had trouble finding a parking space."

"Where did you usually park?"

“Around the corner, on a side street. It was easier than circling around trying to get one of the places in front. And their parking lot is small, crowded.”

“Did you enter the bank through a different door than usual?”

“There’s only one door,” Molly said. “Other than an emergency exit with an alarm bar across it.”

“Did you go directly to the teller’s window? A regular window, correct? Why not the merchant window? After all, the ad agency is a business.”

Molly sighed. “I never liked using the merchant window. Business owners, especially retailers, can have large amounts of cash to be counted. A longer, regular line is often faster. I usually got in the line next to the merchant window”

“And the merchant window was where the thief was standing.”

“Yes.”

“Did you know the teller who was there the day of the robbery?”

Molly frowned, thinking. “I’d been to her window a few times, but I wouldn’t say I knew her. She’d only been working there a month or so.”

“That puts a twist on things,” Bryce said. “Was there anything unusual about her? Was she overly friendly? Talkative? Nervous?”

“Not really,” Molly said. “She was polite, professional. Besides, the police interviewed all the bank employees. If they suspected anyone, they would have pursued it.”

“Not without evidence,” Bryce said. “But you’re right, they were interviewed and cleared.”

“I was cleared, too, supposedly,” Molly pointed out. “Yet, here I am again.”

“Well, that’s because the money is still missing.”

Bryce motioned for more coffee, letting the conversation pause while the cups were refilled. After the server walked away, he leaned forward and continued.

"Tell me what happened when you got to the teller's window."

"It was all very routine," Molly said. "I said hello and handed her the deposit. She said hello back and started to process it."

"And then what happened?"

Bryce watched Molly set her coffee mug down as her hands started to tremble.

"It all blurs together when I replay it in my head. I heard someone gasp – behind me, I think, or maybe to the side. I could hear scuffles and knew others were dropping to the floor, so I did, too. Maybe we were told to get down, I don't remember. Someone was sniffling nearby, scared. I was scared, too. Everyone was."

"How long were you down on the floor?" Bryce asked.

"Only a few minutes, from what others said. It's hard to explain. It's not like a television show, where you see the scene happening and know the details. It was so fast. One moment I was handing the teller my deposit and the next I was on the floor."

Bryce nodded. "Just long enough for the robber to get out of the bank."

"I guess so," Molly said. "After that, a guard helped me up. People were looking around, confused. I left. I just wanted to get out."

"Tell me about the bank robber, anything you can remember," Bryce said. "Are you certain it was a 'she' and not a 'he'," Bryce asked. "Maybe the thief wore a wig as a disguise?"

"The police ruled that out," Molly said. "Something about facial structure."

"Ah, yes," Bryce said. "Facial analysis is fairly accurate, unless someone has had cosmetic surgery. And that wouldn't apply to anyone pulling off a job this small."

"Small?" Molly exclaimed. "You call this small?"

"Relatively," Bryce smiled. "You'd be surprised what goes on that doesn't even reach the news. But let's move on. The bank tapes show the thief dropping below the counter. Maybe you got a closer look at her?"

"No, I didn't look up. I was petrified. And you already know the robber's description from the media coverage." Molly closed her eyes. Was there anything she'd overlooked?

"Someone whispered," Molly said suddenly. "Maybe another customer? I remember hearing the words 'stay down.' It could have been from anyone, but it was close by."

"That could be important, Molly." Bryce's voice grew animated. "No one was able to get a voice from the security tapes. What did it sound like?"

"Deep, sort of raspy," Molly said.

"A woman disguising her voice," Bryce added.

Molly dropped her head into her hands, elbows on the table. "Do you know how many times I've been asked all these questions by the police? Most of the information I have about the robbery is from the news, just like everyone else."

"Yes," Bryce agreed. "But the difference is that you were there."

"Unfortunately," Molly pointed out.

"Tell me about the weeks after the robbery," Bryce said.

Molly looked down, staring into her coffee mug.

"They were awful, a nightmare. After the police released me, it was all over the news. There were news vans in front of my home, reporters on the lawn. I tried to return to work and get back into a routine, but that's when the notes started. The police thought they were pranks. I almost believed them. I *wanted* to believe them. Then my place was broken into and everything was ransacked. That was too much to be someone's idea of a joke."

"But nothing was stolen," Bryce pointed out.

"Right," Molly said with a huff. "That's why the police let it go. They sent a patrol car around for a few nights, but after that I was on my own."

"Do you remember seeing anything strange around your neighborhood - either before or after the robbery?"

Molly paused. "Yes, come to think of it… I didn't see it, but a neighbor said she saw an unfamiliar car parked at the end of our block. She said it was there several days in a row, a few days after the robbery."

"Was this around the time you started getting the notes?"

"Actually, yes." Molly fell silent and then shuddered. "Look, I don't want to talk about this anymore. I just want to forget this ever happened."

"Molly," Bryce said. "You know I think you're innocent. But look at the facts: Even though you weren't involved, the thief's appearance suggested you could be. *That* wasn't coincidental. And the money is still missing. That's why it keeps coming back to you."

Molly slumped back in her seat. "You're telling me this isn't going to go away on its own."

"No," Bryce said. "I'm afraid it isn't."

CHAPTER TWENTY-THREE

Sadie looked over the dessert menu at Eleanor's. Not that she needed anything after the pasta she'd just finished, but the plans she'd been contemplating during the meal had triggered her sweet tooth. This was what they called emotional eating, wasn't it? Eating when you weren't hungry, but because you were upset, sad, angry, or, in this case, excited.

"Does anything look tempting?" the server asked.

"I really shouldn't," Sadie said, not because she meant it, but because it was a handy disclaimer when making a dessert decision.

"Everyone says that," the server said. "But you're on vacation. No calories!"

Sadie laughed. "OK, you talked me into it. I'll have the white chocolate bread pudding with caramel sauce. It sounds delicious! Oh, and I'd like a cappuccino, please."

"Both excellent choices." The server returned to the kitchen.

The decision to have dessert was more about staying at the café. Being away from the inn seemed to clear her head. She was able to look at the situation from a distance. And she was pretty sure by now she knew what she saw.

Bryce and Susie knew each other, but didn't want others to know they did. Why? That was the question. Clearly they hadn't known each other would be there. The surprise on Susie's face was obvious, even though it only lasted a split second. And though Sadie hadn't seen Bryce's face, his voice had altered just enough to show his surprise. Yet each one had snapped out of it instantly. That took practice. Good drama training might accomplish that, but the more she thought about it, the more certain Sadie was that she wasn't the only detective at the inn.

Because of the suspicious way Bryce and Susie had behaved toward each other, Sadie smelled detective on both of them. If Susie was there to find Molly, then her husband was probably in on it, too. Or maybe not. Sadie hadn't ever told Morris what she did beyond her work at the boutique.

Or maybe Susie and Dan *were* a team. That was the problem with this business. No one could ever be sure of anyone.

She closed her eyes as she listed the investigators: Bryce, Susie and possibly Dan. That would leave Mr. Miller as the only guest not involved in the case, which was easy to believe. Not only was he strange, but he kept to himself. He didn't have an investigative bone in his body, as far as she could tell. He was hardly the breakfast conversationalist. Nothing seemed to interest him at all. Traveling salesman was Sadie's best guess – insurance or something equally boring.

"Here you go."

Lost in thought, Sadie was startled by the server's arrival, but delighted when she saw the dessert plate slide in front of her. The bread pudding was a small portion, but every millimeter of it screamed "rich." The caramel sauce crisscrossed the top like a sweet ribbon. It smelled heavenly.

"No calories, you promised, right?" Sadie asked.

"None whatsoever." The server winked and moved on to greet a new table of guests.

Sadie dipped her fork into the bread pudding, carving off a caramel-covered bite. She slipped it between her lips and sighed. It was perfection – warm and sweet. She took a second bite and mulled over her recent thoughts.

Safety in numbers was sometimes a good thing, but, in this case, she doubted it. Only one person was going to get credit – or payment – for finding Molly. With several detectives around, it became a competition, which was a shame. She was rather fond of the other guests. Susie seemed like a sweet girl, though her husband was unimpressive. And Bryce, well, what was there not to like about him? He might as well have stepped out of a Cary Grant movie.

Both Susie and Bryce had believable stories, whether true or not. Susie certainly played the part of a young bride well. Dan was probably just along for the ride. And Bryce – a novelist? Yes, she could see that. Maybe he really was a novelist in his spare time. He wouldn't be the first detective to have a second career going.

A third bite of bread pudding filled Sadie's mouth as she thought over the coincidence of them being at the inn at the same time. She'd never joined forces with other detectives, always preferring to work on her own. This was a unique situation. It was possible she was the only one who had all the dots connected. Bryce and Susie almost certainly knew each other. Her powers of observation were keen. She rarely missed details, one benefit of working alone. It was easier to get distracted with others around. That had been an issue on occasion with Morris, who loved to travel. She'd usually been able to persuade him to let her go on an "independent woman's trip," in order to concentrate on assignments. Now and then, he'd gone along.

The challenge now was how to use the current situation to her advantage. She could stick to herself or maybe pull

Susie under her wing. After all, the girl was young and would probably welcome the help. But that felt risky. Youth didn't necessarily equal naivety. It would be wiser to keep her as a shopping partner. She could keep an eye on the young detective at the same time.

As she sipped her cappuccino, she turned her thoughts to Bryce. It might be worth confiding in him and working on the case together, if he agreed to team up. That was a tough call, though. For one thing, she could be wrong about him being a detective. And if she opened up about her own reason for being there, it could be awkward or dangerous or both. A better tactic would be to get him to open up first, which could be difficult if he was as experienced as she suspected. He would have had plenty of practice keeping his motives to himself. Still, if she could pull it off, joining forces with Bryce could be the best option.

Sadie ate the last of the bread pudding, resisting an uncouth urge to lick the plate. She finished the cappuccino, paid the bill and left the café, waving to a busy Eleanor on the way out.

Indulging in some window-shopping, she strolled down the main street, checking front displays for merchandise that she might have missed on her earlier shopping adventure. She gave herself credit for being thorough. She hadn't missed much, though she noted a turquoise sweater that she might need to try on the next day.

One block from the bed and breakfast, the stores dropped behind her. A cold wind blew across an open field that separated the downtown shopping area from the inn. Without buildings to block the wind, the chilly evening temperature was registering. She picked up her pace. Almost to the inn, Sadie slowed down as she spotted a car pulling up in front. Stepping out of sight, she watched two figures get out of the car and enter the inn. Was she imagining it? No, she wasn't. It was Molly and Bryce.

Sadie waited several minutes before entering the inn herself. She had too much running through her mind to risk conversation. She watched the light in the front, second floor room turn on, envious of Bryce's accommodations. She'd asked for that room when she first called to make a reservation. The ocean view looked spectacular from the website photos.

Molly was nowhere in sight when Sadie stepped into the entry hall, exactly as she'd hoped. She eased the front door closed and went to her room for the night.

CHAPTER TWENTY-FOUR

Susie stretched across the four-poster bed in the barn suite. She hated the old flannel pajamas that she brought on trips with Dan. They were dull and boring, but anything she could do to make him keep his hands to himself was worthwhile. On the positive side, they were comfortable – far more comfortable than some of the itchy lace she'd sported on occasion. And comfort was what she craved after topping off her honey-balsamic glazed salmon fillet at Ocean with chocolate espresso cheesecake.

It wasn't difficult keeping him at arm's length. He pushed constantly with verbal hints, but the lines were clear. Her black belt in karate didn't hurt, either. Dan knew there was only so far he could push her before she'd let go with a vicious kick. She'd never had to use such tactics on him, but he knew she was capable. As far as she was concerned, it was one of the reasons he brought her on assignments with him. He was too much of a wimp to handle difficult situations by himself.

She, on the other hand, had been in plenty of tough spots. Moscow had been one such job. It was likely that her skill in fighting off a counterfeiter had been part of what drew Bryce to her. She'd rather attribute it to her more feminine charms, but she knew the truth. Men were attracted to power and strength as much as to pretty faces and sweet smiles.

She flipped through the pages of a fashion magazine, trying to distract herself from her new concern: Bryce. It was clear he had fooled everyone at the inn but her into believing he was just a wealthy novelist. He was an expert bluffer, would have made a great poker player. In fact, maybe he had been one at some point. He'd worked so many jobs; it was almost certain he'd been in gambling casinos while tracking people down.

Having him in Cranberry Cove posed a big problem. Now, not only did she need to find the money herself, she had to keep him from interfering. And that would be tricky. He was good at what he did – at everything he did, as she remembered too clearly. She tried not to think about those cold Moscow nights that were anything but cold with him around.

Her concentration was interrupted by the sound of Dan gargling in the bathroom. Really! Who gargled, anyway, much less when others could hear? Next he'd be out doing his evening stretches in the sitting area, reaching over his toes while outfitted in striped pajamas. Then he'd start on jumping jacks, as if he were in high school gym class. Finally, he'd pull out the sofa bed – he did know his place, after all – and read one of his old Sherlock Holmes books. It would likely be his fourth or fifth time through the same book. His routine bored her to tears. But it would be worth suffering with it once she got her hands on the money.

This was another disadvantage to having Bryce around. He was undoubtedly there to take Molly back to Tallahassee. But if he took her away immediately, the bed and breakfast would close and Susie's hopes of finding the money would disappear. She needed to find it quickly.

She didn't believe for a minute that the money wasn't there, as Bryce had suggested. He really thought Molly was innocent? That was just like Bryce – getting blind-eyed when working on a case that involved a female. This bothered her, though there was no reason for it to. She'd gotten over their fling a long time ago. Still, it made her nervous that he seemed sure of Molly's innocence. She hated to admit it, but he had good instincts. He was a success at his job, which meant it was possible she was wrong about the money. In that case, Dan would go away without a case solved, which wasn't a big deal, not to her. But she'd go home empty-handed, with nothing in her pockets except memories of enduring another assignment with Dan. That wasn't an outcome she was willing to accept.

Setting aside the magazine, she stared at the ceiling and tried to replay the security tape footage in her head: Molly at one teller's window, the other figure at the next window, Molly, once up off the ground, leaving in one direction, the other figure running in the opposite direction. Chaos both inside and outside the bank made the tapes even more confusing. Aside from the visual clues, there were spoken and written clues from the news reports. Those couldn't always be trusted, she reminded herself. Not the way the media twisted stories around. But the basic facts were there. Molly had been arrested shortly after the robbery and then released after analysis of the tapes indicated she wasn't identical to the suspect. But that didn't prove she didn't have the money. It only proved they had no concrete evidence.

She felt sorry for the young woman, to tell the truth, now that she'd met her. She was a nice person, the kind a guy might take home to meet his mother or the kind that a girlfriend might go out with for tea. But Molly's routine trips to the bank had made her an easy decoy. As they say, wrong place, wrong time – or right place, wrong time – or, whatever the saying was. Or was it actually right place, right time? Was Molly in on it from the start? Wouldn't that be a twist?

That was something she hadn't considered. In a backstabbing world, it was impossible to trust anyone. What a perfect decoy that would be – someone who seemed innocent, but was actually a cover for the crime. No, it was unlikely. Bryce could be right, as much as she hated to give him the benefit of the doubt.

"Anything interesting up there on the ceiling," Dan asked, as he came out of the bathroom. "You know, like clues or money or anything?"

"Very funny," Susie said. "I don't see you coming up with anything."

"Well, if I could solve cases alone, I wouldn't need to bring you with me," Dan said, stretching his arms forward over his toes.

"You'd bring me, anyway."

"True," Dan admitted. "It's just not the same out on the road without you." He started in on the first of many jumping jacks.

"I agree," Susie added, rolling over so she didn't have to watch him. "It's *not* the same without you."

"We need... to come up...with something concrete...now that we're here," Dan said, sputtering words between jumps. "We tracked her....here, but...that doesn't help...without proof."

"Save your breath for your exercises," Susie said. "I already know what you're going to say. You're not sure she's the one with the missing money."

"Yep," Dan wheezed.

Susie sighed. "Well, I'm sure. I never would have agreed to come out to this hokey town if I hadn't been convinced. But we need proof."

"The money," Dan said. "That's the proof." He paused and leaned forward, hands on his knees, catching his breath. "We need to find the money and turn her in."

"Don't worry," Susie said. "I fully intend to find it."

CHAPTER TWENTY-FIVE

After she ran through the routine of preparing for the next morning's breakfast, Molly took the cordless business phone with her into her room at the back of the inn just in case any of the guests needed anything during the night. Once she closed the door to her room, she felt weak from the relief of having time to herself. Her mind was reeling and her body begged for a hot shower and the comfort of her bed. She was mentally and physically exhausted. Tossing a nightshirt on the bed, she disrobed, turned on the shower and stepped under the steaming water. She leaned forward to let the heat soak into her neck and shoulders and let her thoughts wander.

She didn't know how to process what Bryce had told her. The revelation in the kitchen had been so unexpected, she could barely follow it. Her first thought was to run, but it wasn't rational. She hadn't done anything wrong. Besides, she was done running. Aunt Maggie had given her a second chance and she was determined to make it work. If trusting a stranger was going to help, she needed to force herself to do so.

They had chosen the coffee shop on the outskirts of town as a place to continue the kitchen conversation without being overheard. It was a much less popular place than the trendy restaurants and cafés that had been popping up all over town. The run down eatery had few customers so it was more private than other establishments. With only one cook in the kitchen and the server plugged into her iPod, they could talk freely without worry of discovery.

Certainly other situations might have made for a nicer evening out with Bryce – a candlelit dinner at an ocean side bistro or a stroll along the beach, for example. But it was what it was. Without the bank robbery fiasco forcing her to focus, Molly doubted she'd be able to concentrate around Bryce. The silver lining to the whole mess was that Bryce's matter-of-fact attitude helped relax her.

She'd always known someone might follow her across the country. Moving to Cranberry Cove was never about going into hiding, but was simply about leaving the stress of Tallahassee behind. The media had backed off and the police had cleared her. She'd even half-believed them when they said the threatening letters were only a prank. The break-in at her apartment could have been a foolish teenage joke. But it didn't matter. Her calm, uneventful life had been over as soon as she'd become part of the news.

The bed and breakfast had provided a respite from the chaos of her life in Florida, though she always knew deep down that the mess wasn't over. But she hadn't expected bed and breakfast guests to be part of the ordeal. A phone call from the Tallahassee police, maybe. A request for another written statement, maybe. But not someone posing as a guest and then blindsiding her with the story that Bryce had laid out for her.

Molly stepped out of the shower with more questions than answers. Although the hot water had relaxed her body, it did nothing to soothe her mind. She towel dried her hair, put on the nightshirt, climbed into bed and picked up a book from her nightstand. But she couldn't read. Her brain wouldn't stop running through the events of the evening. She turned off the light, hoping the softness of her pillow might lull her to sleep. It didn't work.

She threw on a robe, went to the kitchen and put water on to boil. A cup of Chamomile tea sometimes did the trick when she couldn't sleep. It had worked back in college when she was under the pressure of final exams. It had worked at times when the activity level at the ad agency had been high and she found herself going over work tasks at home. It was worth a try.

Late nights in the kitchen alone always provided a break from stress. It was unusual for guests to leave their rooms at night. Either they had already turned in or were still out for late dinners or, if on a weekend, the occasional concerts that were offered at the town's art center. The dimmed dining room lights usually sent them upstairs as soon as they returned to the inn. After-hour solitude in the inn's back area was one of the perks of business ownership. For exactly this reason, she gasped as she turned back to exit the kitchen and found Bryce standing in the door.

"Sheesh!" she exclaimed. "Do you always make dramatic entrances like this?" The hot tea sloshed over the side of her mug and onto her hand. She moved it to the other hand and shook the one that had been holding it.

Bryce crossed the kitchen and grabbed a towel, turning back to hand it to her. Since dinner, he'd rolled up the sleeves of his flannel shirt. Molly took in the tanned skin of his forearms and the glimmer of light that bounced off his watch. She paused long enough for Bryce to approach and wrap the towel around her hand.

"I apologize," Bryce said. "I didn't mean to startle you, but I was worried. I know everything we talked about came as a shock."

"I'd call that an understatement," Molly managed. Her surprise at finding him in the doorway had eased and she was beginning to feel calmed by his presence. It was an odd sensation, being calmed by someone who brought troubling news.

"You look cute, by the way," Bryce added.

Molly cringed, suddenly recalling her tussled, wet hair, nightshirt and bathrobe. All she needed was a pair of bunny slippers to match Susie's and the look would be complete.

"Very funny," Molly said.

"I'm serious," Bryce said. His smile was genuine. Again, Molly felt calmer. There was something about him that set her nerves at ease.

"Have some tea, as long as you're down here," Molly said. "I couldn't sleep. Sometimes it helps." She moved to the counter and started to pull a mug out of the cupboard.

"I'm more of a coffee drinker, myself," Bryce said, "but don't fix any. It keeps me awake at night."

"Decaf, maybe," Molly offered, holding the mug up as a question.

Bryce shook his head. "I have a secret stash of brandy in my room. That's more my type of evening drink. Would you like some? I hear it goes well with tea."

"You're making that up," Molly said.

"Yes, I am," Bryce laughed. "But that doesn't mean it isn't true."

Molly paused, impulse getting the better of her. "You know, I think I might just have some." What would it hurt? Everything was so confusing already there was no point in trying to keep her regular evening routine.

"I'll be right back, in that case," Bryce said. He left the room and returned shortly with a bottle of Courvoisier VSOP.

"You have good taste, I see," Molly said. She reached into a far cabinet and pulled out a snifter.

"Ah, you're a brandy type of girl after all," he teased.

"No," Molly admitted. "I'm more of a Chamomile tea girl, as you see. But the execs at the job I had in Tallahassee did a lot of entertaining. I kept the in-office bar stocked with their clients' favorite drinks."

"You were a regular at Wine and Spirits, right? Twice a month? You usually checked out with a delightful young lady named Ruth who shared your love of Jane Austen novels. And Chardonnay."

Bryce smiled at Molly's shocked expression. "I followed your trail before I came to California. It's what I do."

Molly sighed, exasperated. "Do you know everything about me?"

"More than you'd like me to know, I imagine," Bryce said. "But not as much as I'd like to."

Was he flirting? Was it a work-related comment? Maybe it was both. Molly was intrigued, flattered and nervous, all at once.

Molly watched as Bryce poured an inch of brandy into the snifter. She didn't stop him when he added brandy to her mug, as well.

"Not too much," Molly cautioned. "I do have to serve breakfast in the morning."

"Ah," Bryce said. "What are we having?" He smiled as he toasted her mug of tea and lifted the snifter of brandy to his lips. Molly could sense his suppressed laughter.

"Dry toast and prunes." Molly smirked.

"My favorite," Bryce answered. There was an unmistakable gleam in his eye.

"I'm afraid you'll be disappointed, then," Molly said, shaking her head. "That's what we have on Sundays for brunch. Tomorrow you're stuck with raspberry French toast, fresh-squeezed juice, cranberry applesauce, lemon-poppy muffins and cranberry nut bread."

"My loss," Bryce threw back. "Good thing I'm here for a week. I get to try all your specialty dishes, dry toast and prunes included."

Great, Molly thought. It was enough that she was wrapped up in the bank robbery again. But the man who was working to help her clear her name was attractive and *flirting* with her. This could be trouble.

It had been two years since her last relationship, and that had ended badly. She blamed herself, having broken her rule of not getting involved with clients. Why the marketing director for the small coffee roasting company had gotten the better of her, she wasn't sure except that she had a weakness for men with smooth moves who seemed sincere.

Like the one who sat across from her now.

She'd been fortunate that her bosses had never realized she'd been seeing the client. When she ended the relationship – and he ended the business association with the company – he'd simply blamed it on his company's budget. It was a classy move, she had to admit. Still, it kept her from dating for a while. And then the bank robbery chaos happened. Since then, dating had been the last thing on her mind.

Molly turned her attention back to Bryce, who was quietly watching her. Again he lifted the brandy snifter to his lips, still not saying a word.

"I just wish this whole thing would blow over," Molly said. "The police were satisfied I wasn't involved. They haven't even contacted me since I've been in Cranberry Cove."

"That only means they couldn't prove anything," Bryce said. "Lack of evidence, that type of thing."

"Great!" Molly exclaimed. "Now you think I did it."

"That's not what I'm saying at all," Bryce said. "I'm just pointing out the police perspective. Look at it from the crooks' viewpoint, too. They've gotten away with crimes in the past. They know it's possible to fool the police."

"I don't understand why anyone would suspect me, anyway," Molly said. "I'm just a plain, everyday girl who was working an everyday job."

"Not so plain," Bryce said. He swirled his brandy around in the snifter and smiled.

"Flattery will get you nowhere with this," Molly said, though she felt herself blush. "Besides, getting back to the subject, there were plenty of other people in the bank that day. Why suspect me? Why not go chasing the others down?"

"Molly, we've been over this already," Bryce said. "It's pretty clear why the attention has been directed at you."

Molly was on the verge of yelling, but kept her voice low, remembering there were guests in the inn. "I know – they stalked me, knew my schedule, planned it to make it look like I did it. But that should make it even more obvious that I wasn't involved."

"Or…all the better for your cover," Bryce said. "You could have been in on it from the beginning, planned it with the thief."

"That is just insane," Molly said.

"You're going to have to think like a criminal in order to get out of this," Bryce said.

"No, *you* are going to have to think like a criminal," Molly said. "*You* tracked me down here. *You* get me out of this."

Molly dropped her head into her hands. When she looked up, Bryce was smiling again.

"What?"

"Your hair is dripping on the table," he said.

"Now you're going to tell me you have a weakness for wet hair?" Molly said. "You know, like some men like blondes and others like brunettes?"

"I'm an equal opportunity hair admirer," Bryce countered.

"How do you live like this?" Molly said. "Always suspicious, never trusting anyone."

"It's just part of the job. If I trust anyone completely, I rule out options. Once that happens, I risk overlooking possibilities, which makes it harder to solve cases."

"I wouldn't want to look at life that way," Molly said. "I need to believe that people are good - innocent until proven guilty. Like *me*, for one perfect example!"

"Yes, like you."

"I just want this all to go away. I don't understand why this keeps coming back to haunt me," Molly said.

"I know. And I do believe you're innocent," Bryce said. "We'll figure this out." He poured another snifter of brandy and started to add more to Molly's tea. She shook her head to stop him and stood up.

"I can't think about it anymore tonight," Molly said. "It's already late and I do have to serve breakfast in the morning."

"Dry toast and prunes?" Bryce laughed as he stood and picked up his brandy.

"If you insist." Molly smiled as she pointed to the door.

CHAPTER TWENTY-SIX

Sadie was the first to arrive at breakfast in the morning, gussied up in an ankle-length lilac skirt and purple tunic with rhinestones on the sleeves. A white velour band with matching rhinestones stretched across her forehead. She poured a mug of coffee at the side buffet and took a seat at the table as Molly entered the room.

"I approve of the flower arrangement, Molly – it matches my outfit. I've always loved purple and white together. And snapdragons with carnations – what a sweet mix!" Sadie added creamer to her coffee and watched Molly place a basket of lemon-poppy muffins at one end of the table and a tray of cranberry nut bread at the other. She grabbed a muffin immediately. "These are still warm – how divine! I may have to eat them all myself."

"That's one advantage of being the first one to breakfast." Molly smiled, but her voice lacked the enthusiasm of someone wide awake.

"Are you feeling ok, dear?" Sadie asked.

Before Molly could answer, Bryce arrived. His khaki slacks and blue button-down shirt gave him a business-like appearance. His hair was still damp from a morning shower. A scent of pine and spice followed him into the room.

"Good morning, Bryce," Sadie said. "I was just asking Molly if she was feeling OK." She turned her attention back to Molly. "Are you, dear?"

Bryce answered for her. "I imagine it can be a handful taking care of a group of guests."

"Yes, it can be," Molly answered, looking at Bryce with a pointed expression. "But I love it," she added quickly, directing the additional comment toward Sadie. "And I feel fine, don't worry. I'm just a bit tired."

Sadie reached for a basket of muffins and handed them to Bryce.

"Try one, they're delicious!"

"Gladly." Bryce reached into the basket and took a muffin, placing it on a bread plate.

"You must get up very early to bake these," Sadie said to Molly before turning back to Bryce. "Put some raspberry jam on that." She waved her hand in the direction of a bowl of preserves. "It's a perfect blend of flavors, the lemon and raspberry."

"Did someone say raspberries?" Susie sashayed into the room, her ponytail as bouncy as the ruffled skirt she wore. Firm, tan legs stretched from the skirt's hem down to a pair of tan flats. Sadie guessed she'd been a high school cheerleader, maybe even homecoming queen. Susie was exactly the kind of girl she'd envied in school.

"Raspberry jam, not raspberries," Sadie said, "but just as delicious. You must try some on these muffins – wonderful!"

"Good morning, Susie," Bryce said. Sadie studied the expression on Susie's face. She didn't seem overjoyed to see him. Perhaps she'd thought she could slide in and out for breakfast before he arrived, just as she'd done the day before.

"Where is that lucky fellow," Bryce continued, "the new husband?"

"Right behind me," Susie said, just as Dan stepped into the room.

"Dan, you know Sadie from yesterday morning," Susie said. "But you haven't met Bryce." She turned what seemed like an exaggerated smile toward Bryce.

"Bryce, this is my husband, Dan."

Bryce leaned forward, extending his hand toward Dan. "Pleased to meet you," he said. Dan returned the handshake politely.

Watching the interaction, Sadie felt certain that Bryce and Dan were meeting for the first time. But Bryce and Susie's reactions to each other still seemed more familiar than new acquaintances.

Molly brought a pitcher of fresh-squeezed juice from the kitchen and set it in the middle of the table, a bowl of cranberry applesauce along with it. "You must have all coordinated your breakfast times," Molly said, a light tilt to her voice.

Susie laughed. "Not really!" She chose the seat next to Bryce. Dan sat on her other side. "Just a coincidence. There are so many unexpected coincidences in life." She turned toward Bryce and smiled. "Don't you think?"

"Absolutely," Bryce countered. His smile was less forced than Susie's. If the two were playing a cat and mouse game, he was winning. Dan seemed oblivious. He stood, reached for the pitcher of juice and poured two glasses.

Molly, on the other hand, had paused at Susie's comment about coincidence. Sadie was growing more and more convinced that there were several scenarios playing out at the table. The trick was to figure out what they were.

"Everyone OK with French toast?" Molly asked.

"Sounds delicious!" Sadie exclaimed. "And we have everyone here…no, that's wrong. You have one more guest staying here – the quiet man from yesterday morning."

"Mr. Miller," Susie said. "Charlie Miller."

"You have a good memory, dear," Sadie said. "I hardly remembered that Mr. Miller *had* a first name."

"I have a better memory than you think," Susie replied. The odd comment was as strange and out of place as Susie's glance toward Bryce.

"Memory can be faulty, you know," Bryce said. "I backpacked in Europe, back in college one summer. It was all the rage, you know?"

He paused to smile at Sadie, who nodded, remembering doing the same thing, although years before Bryce.

"I remember it fondly now," Bryce continued, "perhaps from the viewpoint of missing the 'good old days.' But the reality was that the trip wasn't all that glamorous – finding a hostel for the night, counting change to pick up soup or bread at a corner café. I don't think I had a warm enough jacket – things like that."

"Oh, yes," Sadie jumped in. "I did the same thing. Got stuck in the rain one night in Belgium when I missed a bus, had to walk three miles to get back to the hostel. But, like you said, I remember that time as being wonderful."

"My point being…" Bryce paused to sip his coffee. "…that what we remember isn't the complete picture. Our memory holds onto what it wants to and discards the rest."

"Meaning what, exactly," Susie asked. Sadie thought her voice a bit sharp.

"Meaning the past redefines itself over time," Bryce said. "What we remember isn't always accurate."

Molly brought two plates of French toast from the kitchen. Fresh raspberries and powdered sugar dusted the hot entrée. A serving of scrambled eggs accompanied the dish. She set the plates in front of Sadie and Susie and returned to the kitchen, bringing two more servings out for Bryce and Dan.

"Butter and syrup are in the middle of the table," Molly said.

"The sweeter the better," Bryce said. He reached for the syrup immediately, offering it first to Sadie and then to Susie.

Sadie didn't miss the smile he flashed Molly. Neither did she miss Susie's frown. Or the look that Dan sent to Susie. It was like watching a chain of dominoes.

"Isn't Mr. Miller joining us this morning?" Dan asked.

"He called down to say he'd be skipping breakfast," Molly said. She picked up the breadbasket and headed to the kitchen to refill it with muffins.

"But how could anyone resist this French toast?" Sadie was in heaven, already three bites into the serving. "I might need some of your recipes if they're not secret."

"No problem," Molly laughed as she called over her shoulder. "You'll get a recipe book full of Cranberry Cottage favorites when you check out. And a few dishes from Eleanor's, too. There aren't any recipe secrets around here."

Sadie was sure she heard Dan whisper to Susie, "Just other kinds." Susie shot him a warning look before switching back to her usual sweet smile and looking at Bryce. Sadie focused on a dripping forkful of French toast and syrup. What on earth was going on between the three guests?

"Any plans for shopping today?" Sadie directed the question to Susie, hoping to break the tension in the room.

"Maybe that shoe store a couple streets up," Susie said. "I saw some great boots in the front window – ankle height with three buckles up the side."

"Yes!" Sadie exclaimed. "I saw those, too. They have them in three colors – black, tan and charcoal."

"I'd love a pair of the black…no, make that tan. They're soft and would go with pale colors," Susie said. "Like a camelhair coat in a snow storm, don't you think? Sort of Dr. Zhivago-ish?"

Bryce cleared his throat and took another bite of French toast.

"I have no interest in shopping, do you, Bryce?" Dan said.

"None whatsoever," Bryce said. "A woman's hobby, I think."

"Now, now, you seem like a liberated type," Sadie laughed. "I bet you said that to tease us."

"Yes, I certainly did," Bryce said, though he winked at Dan, who ignored him and took a last bite of breakfast, clearly finding Bryce's gesture annoying. In fact, he seemed to find everything about Bryce annoying.

"Are you done, sweetheart?" Susie set down her fork as she spoke. She looked at Dan brightly. It was clear that Susie expected Dan to be finished when she was.

"Yes, dear," Dan replied. He stood, pushed his chair in and pulled Susie to her feet. Susie's smile faltered briefly as Dan slipped his arm around her shoulder and pulled her close against him.

"Maybe some shops later?" Sadie said. "We could hit that shoe store, if you want."

"Sounds great." Susie said a polite goodbye to Bryce and thanked Molly for breakfast. Hand in hand, the couple left the room to return to the barn suite.

Sadie reached for the tray of cranberry nut bread and offered it to Bryce. He waved it away, indicating that he was full.

"It's none of my business, of course," Sadie said, "but those two seem mismatched to me. He's a quiet sort of guy and she's more...adventurous is the best description, I think – outgoing, alive."

Bryce smiled, but didn't respond. Molly circled the table, refilling both Sadie and Bryce's coffee mugs and removing the plates that Susie and Dan had left.

"Well, young love, new love, what can I say," Sadie sighed. "Those days are long gone for me. I can barely remember that far back."

"Now, Sadie," Bryce said. "It hasn't been *that* many years. And, besides, I bet you can remember plenty about those times."

"Aren't you full of flattery," Sadie said. "But, you're right, I do remember those days. Seems they weren't that long ago, though I know they were."

"What is one favorite memory, Sadie?" Bryce sat back in his chair, his right hand curled around his coffee mug.

Sadie waited while Molly removed their plates and then leaned back with her coffee, thinking over her answer.

"How far back do you want me to go?"

"As far as you want," Bryce said.

"Now that you have me thinking about it, I don't have to go back all that far," Sadie said. "I have many wonderful memories of times with my late husband, Morris. But one that stands out is a charity dance we attended in San Francisco. It wasn't long before he died. He called me one day – from another room in our house, mind you – and asked me out on a date. Those were his exact words. 'Will you go out on a date with me tonight?' It was a cool evening and I wore a green velvet dress that I hadn't worn in years. He greeted me at the front door with a wrist corsage, and we went out to dinner and then danced. There was a marvelous band playing our favorite swing music from the forties."

"It sounds wonderful," Bryce said.

"Yes, it was." Sadie grew quiet, wrapped up in reliving the memory. "We didn't know at that time that he'd be gone soon. At least I didn't. He was always quiet about doctor visits. He had that live day-to-day philosophy. In any case, it was an enchanting evening, one that I'll never forget."

Sadie stood and set her coffee mug on the table, the rhinestones on her sleeves sparkling as the sunlight streamed through the window.

"Thank you for inspiring me to think about it again."

"You're welcome," Bryce said, also standing up. "Memories are good to have."

"I imagine you have a few, too," Sadie smiled.

"Just a few," Bryce said. "Some are good; some I don't care to recall."

"I think we all have a few of those," Sadie said.

"Yes, I imagine you're right about that," Bryce replied.

CHAPTER TWENTY-SEVEN

Susie ran the silk scarf through her fingers, enjoying its soft, cool surface. Its deep blue and green ran together like a forest stream. It was one of several great finds in the last boutique that she'd wandered into while shopping with Sadie. Maybe the town wasn't as boring as she thought. The people were so trusting. It was easy to have an entertaining shoplifting spree.

Patting the side of her shoulder bag, she mentally counted up the day's take so far. The silver bracelet had been so easy it was almost embarrassing. Trying it on and rolling it under her cuff was a tried and true technique. Earrings were always simple to pocket and, with the shop clerk gabbing on her cell phone all the time, Susie had managed to stash four pair in one of her front pockets. The scarf would be a wonderful match to the cashmere sweater she had on under the baggy one she'd worn in. But she knew better than to push her luck. She went to the counter and paid for the scarf. No sense getting caught at something as minor as a hobby. She had yet to accomplish her intended goal, the reason she'd come to Cranberry Cove.

Susie alternated between conversation with Sadie and wandering along clothing racks and jewelry displays. Money wasn't a problem. She had a good amount of savings and could drop a few hundred dollars on any given shopping spree. But where was the fun in that? Anyone could walk up to a counter and buy things. It took talent to shop without spending money. And risk and danger and challenge – all varieties of her favorite drug: adrenalin.

This brought her back to her main purpose. She needed to find the money that Molly had hidden. There was no question in her mind that Molly had it. How the police had managed to miss it when they let her go was a puzzle. She obviously wasn't a pro, but just someone who was in the right place to take advantage of an opportunity. Quiet office girl, indeed. That hadn't fooled her, even following the news broadcasts with the security camera footage. Just as the reserved bed and breakfast owner image didn't fool her now. Looks could be deceiving.

Making excuses that she wasn't feeling well – that raspberry French toast had been SO rich – she left Sadie to shop on her own and returned to the inn. Molly would be out running errands, if she kept to her apparent afternoon routine. Bryce might be at the inn, unless he was out tracking Molly – whether to prove her guilty, prove her innocent or just to flirt with her.

The last thought steamed her. She'd never wanted a permanent relationship. It would only get in the way of her career. But she also didn't like men walking away, especially after they wined and dined her on Russian caviar and champagne. That was just insulting to someone who liked to call the shots herself. Wasn't it fate that they'd ended up on the same assignment again? It should have been a chance to take up where they left off, even for just a few days – or nights. Instead she had a mousy innkeeper standing in her way.

That restaurant called Ocean, where she'd made Dan take her the night before, would be a perfect place for a romantic night out with Bryce. Certainly better than the blasé evening she'd suffered through with Dan. She had to admit the crab cake appetizer with truffle oil was scrumptious. But having to tolerate Dan's chatter and fawning over her for an entire meal was a high price to pay for fine cuisine, no matter how delicious. She reminded herself, not for the first time, to turn down jobs from him in the future. This trip was an exception, one she'd only agreed to because it brought her to Molly on his dime. It was a perfect cover for her real motives, giving her an excuse to be in Cranberry Cove, searching the inn.

But that was enough of her meandering thoughts. She needed to focus. As she walked up the side pathway to the barn suite, she pulled her thoughts back on track.

Dan wasn't in the suite, much to her relief. A note on the coffee table from him was even more reassuring. He'd gone up to the nearest big town and wouldn't be back for a couple hours. Susie smiled to herself. Dan was rarely focused. His habit of heading off on tangents could be annoying, but this time it worked to her advantage. Everyone except Bryce was away from the inn, as far as she knew. With the exception of the second floor, where Bryce's room was located, she could search for the money. The creaky stairs would warn her if he started down to the entryway. Besides, what was it he was doing? Pretending to be a novelist? He would probably hole up in his room for hours.

The barn suite was a dead end, she already knew. She'd searched every inch of it, rummaging through each room when Dan was out of the way. The inn itself was the place to look. And now was the perfect opportunity.

Susie slipped around the back of the main building, entering through the kitchen. Bryce's room was at the front of the inn, looking out at the ocean. If he was there, he would have been able to see her walk up to the front porch. The door to the kitchen allowed her to enter unseen.

Nice to flaunt his money like that, she thought. He picked the deluxe, oversized, ocean-view accommodation. That was one thing that attracted her to him, the fact that money was no object. He could just as easily have taken a smaller room. After all, he was traveling alone. But he did like the finer things in life. Exactly the kind of man she admired.

The kitchen was dark. One window over the sink let light in, but it was small. A side window was even smaller. A four-paned window in the door let in a bit more light, but not much.

Susie searched the kitchen quickly, not knowing how long Molly would be gone. Of all the rooms, it was probably the hardest one to justify being in. Just in case, she had an excuse prepared. Not that saying she needed a vase for flowers would do much good if Molly caught her in a utensil drawer, which is where she started.

Drawer by drawer, she inspected the insides quickly. There were no envelopes or hidden panels. Canisters were her next target, those on the counter, as well as those in cupboards. They all proved to contain cooking supplies – flour, sugar, pasta, coffee and tea bags, but no money. The freezer and refrigerator compartments – a standard but still likely place to hide things – were just as unrewarding. Not to mention that it was tough to keep from breaking a nail while digging through stacks of frozen goods.

After checking walls and cabinets for secret panels, Susie moved on. Molly's room revealed nothing, though she limited her time in there to floorboards and the closet. She'd have no excuse at all if she were caught in there. She could come back if she didn't find the money somewhere else. The dining room was also a bust. Susie wasn't surprised at this.

Hiding something in the most frequented room in the building sounded great for a movie plot, but not smart in reality.

Susie moved to the front hallway and looked around, determining her next step. There were two vacant guest rooms on that floor, plus a small library. Molly's office was only a small alcove off the dining area, so it was easy to check. The library would be time-consuming, but easy to go through at a later hour, since it was intended for guests, anyway. She wouldn't need an excuse to be browsing in there.

She skipped the library and searched the two guest rooms, since their doors were propped open to show the accommodations off to visitors. Both were quaintly decorated and neat, without a lot of frills. She made quick work of checking old-fashioned hatboxes, drawers, floorboards and table bottoms. Nothing turned up.

Wandering back through the hallway, she paused to push against the sides of the main stairway's steps. Though carpeted above, the small, side panels were wood. But they all felt secure as she pushed on them. The same applied to doors and doorjambs, molding and support columns. Nothing indicated any alterations had been made.

A creak upstairs told Susie that Bryce was in the house, as she had suspected. She waited for sounds of a door opening and footsteps on the stairs, but none came. She was half disappointed and half relieved. Of all the people to catch her snooping, he was the least problematic. He knew why she was in Cranberry. It would only be a problem if he caught her with money in her hands. He'd consider the case solved and turn in the money. He'd go for the glory of honesty and offer to split the reward with her to placate her.

It would have been much easier if he hadn't been there at all. That was the biggest problem. Sneaking around Dan was easy, clueless as he was. With Bryce it was challenging. There was no way to check the upstairs floor now, with him in the building, so Susie slipped out the rear door and returned to the suite.

CHAPTER TWENTY-EIGHT

Sadie took her usual seat at Eleanor's, stuffing overflowing bags of purchases into the chair on the opposite side of the table. She'd worked up an appetite while shopping and, as always, Eleanor's felt like home. If she could pack it up in her suitcase and take the café back to San Francisco, she would.

She ordered the day's lunch special, a variation of a Reuben sandwich on fresh-baked multi-grain bread, served with a Greek salad. She added a glass of iced tea to the order and sat back, watching other customers and letting her thoughts wander.

Although Susie seemed sweet, something about her didn't ring true to Sadie, whose instincts were keen, which had helped her solve many cases. Not only was she not imagining the familiar looks between the girl and Bryce, but Sadie was also certain she'd seen Susie pocket items while shopping. She'd thought she imagined it the first time they went shopping together, but not this time. And that didn't fit in with the young, sweet bride image. Yes, something was very off.

In fact, there were a few things that seemed strange about the inn's occupants and their interactions, as far as Sadie was concerned. Susie didn't fit the newlywed image, but neither did Dan. He was too reserved around Susie, as if he wanted to be close to her, but knew better than to push too far. There was some sort of unspoken barrier between them. Most people wouldn't pick up on it, that's how subtle it was. But Sadie wasn't fooled.

Molly had all the qualities an innkeeper should have. She was welcoming, courteous, a great cook, attentive to detail and hospitable without being pushy. She didn't have any qualities that hinted at her being a criminal. Either she was remarkable at hiding her true personality – an Oscar-caliber actress, at that – or she was not the person Binky was looking for. If Sadie were placing bets, she would still be betting on Molly's innocence.

As for the other guests, there wasn't much to surmise regarding Mr. Miller, since he kept to himself. If it was possible for a person to have no personality at all, he fit the bill. But Bryce was another story. He made a point of being present at all available social situations – breakfast and the wine and cheese hour, for example. He read on the front porch and had coffee in the library. He kept himself available to people. Especially to Molly, though that seemed only natural. Molly was attractive and Bryce was traveling alone. It was only logical that he'd create opportunities to talk to her.

But, no, she was sure Bryce was more than a charming lady's man novelist. He was staying close to Molly so that he could observe her. She was as certain of this as she was that several of Binky's detectives had converged on the inn. This certainty made her lose her appetite with the great need to *do* something to bring things to an end.

When the server returned with her sandwich and salad, she asked to have the meal boxed up to go, finished the iced tea and headed back to the inn.

As if she had predicted it, Bryce was in the inn's library when Sadie bustled through the front door, arms laden with shopping bags and the box of food from Eleanor's in one hand. She greeted him by waving with her free hand before going to the kitchen door and knocking. Not getting an answer, she hesitated briefly and then took the liberty of storing her boxed food in the kitchen's refrigerator, something Molly had offered during check-in.

Still hours before the wine and cheese would be set out, pots of coffee and hot water for tea sat on the buffet table. Sadie helped herself to a cup of coffee and returned to the library, sitting down beside Bryce. In his usual, charming manner, Bryce smiled.

"Why, Sadie," he said. "How nice to see you." He lowered his gaze to take in the tissue-stuffed bags that she'd set on the floor beside her. "I take it you've been out shopping again."

"Guilty as charged," Sadie laughed. "What's a getaway weekend without a little retail therapy?"

"Absolutely," Bryce said.

"Is Susie back?" Sadie asked. She set her coffee down and began to rummage through her bags, reminding herself what she'd purchased. One of her guilty pleasures after shopping was taking inventory of everything she bought. It was almost like getting the items as gifts since so many of the items she bought left the sales counters wrapped in tissue paper and tucked into colorful, logo-imprinted bags with handles, just like gift bags.

"Weren't you shopping together?" Bryce said.

"Yes, at first, but she wasn't feeling well and came back here, I thought. I stopped for lunch at Eleanor's." Sadie said. "I just love that restaurant. Wish I could tie it to the back of my car and take it home with me."

Bryce laughed. "I haven't been there, but I keep hearing great things about it. I'll have to try it while I'm here. In any case, I've been upstairs working, so I can't say if Susie's here or not."

"Make sure you try the Reuben sandwich." Sadie pushed the shopping bags to the side and picked up her coffee.

"I'll keep that in mind," Bryce said.

"Working on that novel of yours today, I take it." Sadie offered.

"Trying," Bryce said.

Sadie sat back and blew across the top of her coffee before taking a sip. She determined it wasn't too hot, took a bigger sip and let the cup rest in her lap, hands around the sides. Confronting Bryce with her theory was risky, but the result could be helpful to both of them, if her hunch was right. It was a question of tricking him into revealing his real motives for being in Cranberry Cove. She'd always been good about reading facial expressions. A light discussion that she could back away from was the key. Debating several different conversation starters, she decided on an approach and spoke.

"I don't remember where you're from, Bryce," Sadie said. As she expected, the question caught him off-guard. He set his coffee down and leaned back, crossed his legs casually and let his arms rest on the chair.

"It never came up, if I recall," he said. "I'm from a little bit of everywhere. I don't like to be stuck in one place for too long." The relaxed smile returned as he waited for her response.

Sadie considered saying something about how he and Susie seemed familiar to each other, but thought better of it. Sure though she was, she may have misread the signals between them. He was attractive enough to throw a young woman off guard. Besides, what she was about to hit him with was enough.

"Well, you seem like a man of the world. Let me guess. You're from New York…no, maybe Los Angeles... Or, hey! How about Tallahassee?"

Sadie could have sworn Bryce's tan faded three shades at her question, though he recovered his color within seconds. A true pro, she thought to herself. But her knack for observation outdid his recovery skills.

"Tallahassee?" he replied casually. "Don't know that I've ever been there."

"Neither have I," Sadie said. "I'm not much for humidity and giant bugs, and I hear Florida is overrun with both. Why people choose to retire there is beyond me, but 'to each his own,' as they say. I do know people there."

"You don't say." Bryce leaned forward and rested his forearms on his knees. His smile remained, but he seemed cautious, focused.

Sadie was tempted to leave him hanging for a minute, just for the thrill of having the upper hand. But Bryce seemed like a nice guy. It wouldn't be fair. And she didn't care that much about having the upper hand.

"I have a sense that you're growing rather fond of our little innkeeper," Sadie said. "I don't blame you. She seems sweet. She also seems, if I may use a legal term, innocent."

Bryce's smile faltered and he raised his eyebrows, but he said nothing, just listened, cool as could be.

"Oh, don't worry. I know why you're here, but I'm not going to cause any trouble. And I don't care about the reward money," Sadie said. "I just came up here because it was a chance to get away for the weekend, and my old friend Binky asked me to help him solve a … problem." Sadie took a sip of coffee, enjoying the confused look that was plastered across Bryce's face.

"Binky?" Bryce repeated. "Did you say 'Binky'?"

Sadie laughed, realizing how silly the nickname sounded. She never thought twice about it. A forty-year-old habit was hard to break.

"Oh, my," she said, "that must sound ridiculous! I've called him that for so many years I forget he has any other name. You probably know him as Al. But he'll always be Binky, my ex-husband, to me."

"I thought your husband's name was Morris," Bryce said, confused.

"It was," Sadie said. "Morris was my third husband. Seymour was my second. Binky was my first."

Bryce leaned back in his chair, watching Sadie with a perplexed look. He remained quiet as he put the pieces together and then burst out laughing.

"Sadie…" he said, "You're *that* Sadie? The love of Al's life? The mysterious Sadie that we've heard about for years?"

"The one and only," Sadie said, grinning. "Well, maybe not the only – who ever really knows – but definitely the one."

"No," Bryce assured her. "You're the only Sadie as far as he's concerned. But…I don't understand how this ties together."

"It's actually not that complicated," Sadie said. "We were childhood sweethearts, grew up in Brooklyn together. We married right out of high school – against both our parents' wishes, I might add. What can I say, we were young and in love."

"And then?" Bryce prompted.

Sadie sighed, shook her head slowly.

"I haven't thought about this for a long time," she said. "We were naive, at least I was. He ran with a tough crowd, but always kept me shielded from it. Eventually, that was why we separated and divorced."

"Because you wanted a better life," Bryce said.

"No, it was the other way around," Sadie said, smiling. "He wanted a better life for me, said that he was involved with family business that wasn't good for me to be around."

"He cared about you," Bryce said. "He wanted you to be safe."

"I didn't think so at first, of course," Sadie said. "I was young and in love and angry and hurt. But, in time, I saw that he was right. And that he'd given me a gift by setting me free."

"Yet, you've stayed in touch."

Sadie laughed. "Yes, from a distance. He knows I like puzzles, so he tosses me a case to solve now and then. I'm good at observing things."

"So I've noticed," Bryce said.

"But never mind Binky," Sadie continued. "That's not the reason I brought this up. Let's talk about Molly."

"OK," Bryce said, his expression guarded.

"She doesn't have the nature to be involved with something like this, at least not on purpose," Sadie said. "I think she was just an easy decoy for whoever planned that robbery. And then it backfired. She became the suspect while the real thief got away."

Bryce lifted his coffee mug, buying time by taking a drink. Sadie knew she'd thrown a lot at him, expecting him to trust that her motives were sincere. It would take a leap of faith for him to join forces with her. She was relieved when he leaned forward and spoke up.

"I think she's innocent, too," he said. "I'm just trying to figure out how to prove it."

"Well, maybe two detectives are better than one, in this case," Sadie said. "No pun intended," she added.

"I think you're right," Bryce said. "When do we start?"

"I say right now," Sadie said.

CHAPTER TWENTY-NINE

The "open" sign on the front door of Casey's Hardware Store swayed as Mr. Miller walked in.

"Good afternoon, sir." The clerk smiled as he swept a broom across the shop floor. "Can I help you find something?"

Obnoxious fellow, Mr. Miller thought as he closed the door behind him. There's no good reason to be that cheerful on a workday. If he'd wanted to be verbally accosted, he could have hung out at the inn. Thank goodness he'd gotten out of there. Any more social interaction with those guests would've been more than he could handle.

"Paint supplies are on sale, twenty percent off. We've got brushes and rollers on one side of Aisle 6, with drop cloths, rags and masking tape on the other side. Good time to stock up if you have any projects coming up."

"I don't," Mr. Miller stated. He peered at the clerk's nametag. "Casey," just like the name of the store. Probably the owner.

"We've got a special on garden tools, too. Buy two trowels and you get a cultivator for free." Casey lifted a hand and made a claw shape.

"No, thank you," Mr. Miller said.

Didn't the flat tone in his voice make it obvious to the man that he didn't need suggestions? When he was ready to make a purchase, he would – not before and not after.

Mr. Miller wandered up and down the aisles, methodically covering one side of displays before turning back to peruse the opposite side. Each time he rounded a corner, he encountered a new category of merchandise – bathroom fixtures, tools, outdoor equipment, camping gear, and on and on. The variety of products unsettled him, just as it did when he visited any store. He could never work in a place like Casey's. The sheer thought of keeping that much inventory tidy and orderly practically gave him hives.

He paused in the picnic supply area. As with every other department in the store, there were too many items. Barbecue sets served a purpose, he could see, but why should there be two dozen kinds, decorated with everything from fake antlers to sports team logos? Whatever happened to plain old functional tools?

He moved on, pausing in front of a section devoted to fishing gear. Now that was something he would enjoy – sitting on a boat, floating on a lake, alone, no one to bother him. That image was comforting. He wondered why he hadn't yet taken up fishing. Well, there was the part about killing the fish that he found messy and disconcerting. But, aside from that, the solitude of the sport appealed to him.

"How much for the containers with latches on them," Mr. Miller asked. From a center aisle, he pointed back down the row of fishing supplies.

"The tackle boxes?" Casey paused his sweeping and looked up. "Those aren't on sale."

"That was not my question. I asked how much they cost."

Casey frowned, taken aback by the customer's brusque manner. "The tackle boxes are twenty-nine dollars."

Mr. Miller vanished down the aisle of fishing gear and reappeared moments later with two tackle boxes, one in each hand, which he placed on the front counter. Casey set the broom aside and took a place at the cashier's stand.

"I'll take these two," Mr. Miller said, pulling several bills from a bi-fold wallet.

"Good choices, there. Double-sided latches, deep trays and worm-proof compartments. Those'll last you a long time – great quality. Good idea to buy a back-up, too."

"Only one is for me."

"Ah, you must be giving one as a gift. Very smart," Casey said, his eyes lighting up. "People don't realize how a common item can be just as exciting as something fancy. Not that I'd give my sweet Eleanor fishing gear as a surprise, but that's because she doesn't like to fish. Otherwise, I'm sure..."

"How much do I owe you?"

"Fifty-eight dollars plus tax," Casey said, ringing up the purchase on the store's register. "I'll run two receipts – one for you to keep and one for our weekly raffle."

"I'm just passing through," Mr. Miller said.

"The drawing ends this evening," Casey said.

"I'm checking out in the morning." Mr. Miller took his change and receipt, picked up one tackle box in each hand and left the store.

"You could win twenty dollars," Casey shouted after him. He shook his head, tossed the duplicate receipt in the raffle jar and went back to sweeping.

****

The racket that greeted Mr. Miller as he stepped into the inn was unendurable. So much chattering! Even if he hadn't needed to run up to the hardware shop, he would have wanted to hide out in his room. How could people even gather their senses together when surrounded by such verbal disorder? This was why he preferred to stay in motels and chain hotels when he traveled. He could get by with a room key and a pair of earplugs. He didn't bother anyone and no one bothered him. Exactly the way he liked it. This was the first and last time he'd stay at an annoyingly friendly place like Cranberry Cottage Bed and Breakfast. Fortunately, he was certain he wouldn't need to.

He climbed the stairs, doing his best not to cause the boards to squeak. Even if they did, the boisterous crowd below would likely drown out the sound. He locked himself in his room and placed one of the tackle boxes on the bed. The other remained in the trunk of his car.

Pulling his briefcase out, he set it next to the tackle box and opened it. He moved the thin notebook onto the desk along with a crisp sheet of formal stationery. He set his favorite pen next to it in preparation for the letter he intended to write before checking out of the inn. From a zippered compartment, he took out a pair of thin, latex gloves. No self-respecting detective would travel without those. Besides, he'd learned his lesson the day of the robbery.

He pulled a nail file from a second pocket and jimmied the bottom panel of the briefcase and lifted it towards him, exposing the hidden compartment that had served him well on this trip. Lined up carefully, side by side, were banded stacks of hundred dollar bills.

Sixty thousand dollars, he thought, as he began to transfer the bills into the tackle box. It was a lot of money. More than he'd ever seen at one time. More than enough to boost his retirement funds and help him start a new life. And, as far as he was concerned, the sooner he got rid of it, the better.

He hadn't even been looking to change his life until that day at the bank in Tallahassee. Boring had always been acceptable to him. He'd never craved the limelight, never minded his Friday night frozen dinners in front of television. Why, if he'd been looking to live on the edge, he would have stuck around the bank after looking in the front window and seeing the customers on the marble floor. After all, what could be more exciting than haphazardly walking in on a bank robbery? That was the stuff of movies. He could have watched from the front window and still gotten away.

Instead, he'd fled around the corner like a scared kid and then doubled back when he saw the suspicious car parked in the alley. How was he to know that the thief would careen around the corner at that very second, heading for the getaway car? But that's the way it happened. One minute he was backing away from a suspicious scene inside the bank. Sixty seconds later he was standing in an alley, a thief knocked out cold on the ground, a getaway car fleeing and a bag of money in his hands.

What could he do?

His first instinct was to stand still and wait for the authorities to come. It wouldn't be that hard to explain, would it? That he just happened to be in the alley, accidentally knocked out a thief, scared off a getaway car and stood around waiting for help? As if that would be a believable story.

His second instinct was to drop the money and take off. But that could have been a problem, since his fingerprints were now on the bag. And the thief could wake up at any moment. She could blame him or – worse – do away with him altogether.

So he followed his third instinct. He ran.

Only hours later, watching the news, did the enormity of the situation sink in. He sat on the couch in his doublewide trailer, the bag of cash on his lap and a chicken potpie on top of the bag. His eyes were glued to the television set and it wasn't even his usual episode of *Jeopardy*. What was this girl thinking, holding up a bank like that? Or were there two girls involved? It was hard to tell by watching the security tapes, even with the news channels playing them over and over.

He was certain he'd only crashed into one girl when he tried to turn back in the alley. At least there was only one girl on the ground when he stood up. Newscasts indicated the same theory, that only one person had pulled off the robbery, that the other girl had been an innocent decoy. The story had gone back and forth for days stretching into weeks. The girl was arrested, the girl was released, the girl was innocent, but had left town. He watched each newscast with renewed curiosity, night after night, the bag of cash on his lap, a different frozen dinner on top.

Now, moving the money from his briefcase to the tackle box, he counted his blessings. He was only a small-town detective, after all. This was a big case, much bigger than chasing runaway dogs or finding out who was stealing newspapers from driveways. The payout he would receive for finding this bank robber would make life easy for some time. And the best part of it all was he didn't even have to go claim it. He could solve the crime, get himself out of trouble and get compensated without speaking to anyone, other than the bare minimum conversation he had to endure when passing other guests at the inn.

He snapped his briefcase closed and locked it, placing it next to the desk. Closing the tackle box, he latched it tight and paused to consider his options. He cracked the door to his room slightly. Hearing guests still tossing around mindless chatter downstairs, he closed it again.

Hours passed before the ruckus of the wine and cheese hour quieted down. Stepping into the hallway, Mr. Miller descended the stairs and paused in the front hallway, hearing only silence. He borrowed a flashlight from a front hallway utility closet and left the building, tackle box in hand.

The inn had a clear view of the pathway that led to the Cottage Suite and rear garden, but Mr. Miller's destination was on the opposite side of the building. Secluded and dark, there was little chance of being watched. To play it safe, he kept the aim of the flashlight low and took cautious, quiet steps.

He'd checked out the property thoroughly when he first arrived, making a mental list of twenty potential hiding places. Narrowing the possibilities down, he'd arrived at a final decision between two locations, one inside the inn and one outside. His initial leaning was toward the library. Access to it during the middle of the night seemed a safe bet, especially if he locked the door behind him. He could always say that he couldn't sleep and was looking for something to read. But the discovery of the tackle boxes at the hardware store that morning had swayed him toward another option.

Tackle box in hand, he walked around the far side of the building, stopping halfway to the back, in front of a metal tool shed. Setting the box on the ground, he flipped the latch to the side and pulled one door open. This was the part that had been the hardest when he had first inspected the shed. Haphazard stacks of pots, tools, dirt-covered gloves and hose nozzles littered the warped shelving, all out of order. The chaotic display unnerved him, but it didn't matter. The task wouldn't take more than a minute and then he'd finally be free.

He pulled a bag of potting soil forward, flinching as an ant ran across the side. He found the thought of grabbing the bag with his hands revolting, even with the latex gloves on. It was bad enough that he'd have to scrub his hands after he removed the gloves, not only to get rid of any grime, but in case any pesticides or chemicals had settled inside. After a short struggle to move the bag forward, he placed the tackle box behind it and pushed the bag back into place with his foot. He inspected the arrangement. It was perfect. The bag hid the box. The box hid the money. And the money was where it belonged, with the thief, where it should have been all along.

He returned to his room and sat down at the desk, where his favorite pen and stationery waited. Only one brief letter and a good night's sleep remained before his mission would be complete.

CHAPTER THIRTY

Molly cleared the last of the Monday morning breakfast dishes from the table and carried them into the kitchen. Bryce followed, mug of coffee in hand.

"What will the guests think of you being in the kitchen?" Molly said.

"I'm not worried about that," Bryce laughed. "But if *you* are, we can arrange a clandestine meeting under a water tower or maybe with a bottle of wine and blanket out on the bluff."

Molly smiled with her back to him. He was breaking down her defenses, whether she wanted him to or not. Not only was he attractive, but he seemed like one of the good guys. It had been a long time since she felt she could trust anyone. It felt good, comforting. For the last few months, she'd wondered if she'd ever be able to trust anyone again.

"I'm just giving you a hard time," Molly said. "I don't think the guests will care or even notice. Susie and Dan have their newlywed bliss out in the barn suite, Sadie is undoubtedly on her way shopping again and Mr. Miller is checking out this morning. No one's concerned with what I do after breakfast. This is the time I usually get my office work done, and after checkout, I run errands. Guests don't pay much attention to where I am or who I'm with."

"Any arrivals tonight?" Bryce asked. He emptied his coffee mug and set it on the kitchen counter, leaning over the sink and looking out into the backyard.

"None," Molly said. "We'll just have Sadie and the Jensens for the wine hour, since Mr. Miller is leaving this morning. And they all check out tomorrow."

"Any new guests tomorrow?" Bryce asked. He turned away from the window and leaned back against the counter facing Molly. She felt herself blush. She'd been so caught up in the tension of the bank robbery that she hadn't realized until now that the other guests were checking out; Bryce was staying a few more days; no other guests were due to arrive until the following week. She would be alone in the inn with possible trouble, and not the robber-chasing variety.

"I take that as a 'no.' Then I think a dinner out is in order," Bryce said. "How about tomorrow night?"

"To discuss the case, you mean," Molly said, though she knew the invitation had little to do with the case.

"Of course," Bryce said. His voice was calm.

Molly made the mistake of glancing at him. If she hadn't, she could have missed the teasing grin on his face. The man knew exactly how he affected her. How many women had fallen under his spell in the past? She hated to even guess.

"I was thinking about trying that restaurant called Ocean," Bryce said. "It seems to be the hip place to go around here."

"Well, I don't know if anything around here would be described as 'hip' exactly," Molly laughed. "But Ocean may be as close to 'hip' as it gets in Cranberry Cove."

"You recommend it to guests," Bryce pointed out.

"Yes, I do," Molly said, "because of the feedback I receive when my guests dine there. The comments I get help me to recommend restaurants, stores and interesting sites to future guests. I haven't been to Ocean, but Susie and Dan went there and said it was great."

"Interesting couple," Bryce said. "I'll bet honeymooners make reservations at the inn way in advance."

"They usually do," Molly said. "Though Susie didn't. She only called a few days ago. She told me there was some kind of last minute change in their honeymoon plans. She was delighted I had an opening."

"I imagine she was." Bryce's tone was nonchalant. "Well, some people are quite spur-of-the-moment, I suppose." Molly barely heard him and passed the comment off as unimportant.

"I keep guest books in the rooms where visitors can write down their impressions of the inn and the area. They write down what they liked, what they'd recommend to other guests. It's sort of a bed and breakfast tradition. Quite a few visitors have left positive comments about Ocean."

"I'll have to keep that in mind and add something myself," Bryce said. "So far I'm quite taken with some of the charms of the inn itself."

"You're speaking of the wine and cheese, I'm sure."

"Of course," Bryce said, smiling. "I would come back just for that afternoon social hour. Multiple visits, I believe. In fact, I think I'll plan to do just that."

"Return guests are always welcome at Cranberry Cottage Bed and Breakfast." Molly smiled.

"Maybe some guests are more welcome than others?" Bryce took a step closer to Molly, leaning one elbow on the counter.

Molly closed her eyes as the familiar scent of pine and spice struck her senses.

"Maybe," she admitted. It was getting more difficult to resist the man with every comment he threw out. Still, she stepped back and pulled herself together.

"However," Molly said, "we're still on *this* visit and I believe we have a bank robbery to solve."

"Yes, you're right about that," Bryce said. The switch in his focus was immediate. *He must be very good at solving cases*, Molly thought, watching the serious look wash away the former flirtatious manner. She certainly hoped he was.

"We'll get this figured out, Molly," Bryce said. "I promise."

"I hope so," Molly said. "I hate the feeling I'm on the run when there's nothing I should have to run from."

"So is that a yes for dinner tomorrow night at Ocean?"

"Sure," Molly said. "Why not? And, Bryce…"

"Yes?" He stopped in the kitchen door and looked back at Molly.

"Thank you."

"You're welcome," Bryce said, smiling as he left the kitchen.

Molly turned back to the sink and began to rinse out coffee cups. Thanking Bryce hardly seemed enough, but it was a start. Hopefully he would be able to help. She was innocent, so she had nothing to hide. There was no harm in trusting him because there wasn't anything he could find that would work against her.

Molly sighed. Deep in her heart, she had known that coming to Cranberry Cove wasn't going to end the problems. Still, it had been a good decision. It had given her distance after things fell apart in Tallahassee. Even the few months she'd been running the bed and breakfast had given her a chance to relax and regroup.

She'd been ready for a change, anyway. Fate tended to work in strange ways, one event becoming a catalyst to another. Granted, she would rather have skipped the whole bank robbery scenario. Certainly there could have been less dramatic situations to jumpstart her move. But it had happened the way it had.

Molly finished the last bit of breakfast clean up and moved to her office. She returned a message from the answering machine, an elderly couple looking for a quaint place to stay while starting off on retirement travels. It was one of the things Molly enjoyed most about running the inn, seeing the variety of circumstances that sent people to the area. It was like catching glimpses of personal photo albums. Each stay was a snapshot in time of someone's life.

She heard someone coming down the stairs, and soon found Mr. Miller standing before her desk, room key in hand.

"Checking out, I see," Molly said, handing him a receipt she'd prepared ahead of time, along with the traditional copy of Aunt Maggie's "Cranberry Cottage Cookbook."

"Yes, I'm leaving now," Mr. Miller said. He set the room key down and took the receipt. He rejected the cookbook with a quick shake of his head.

Molly picked up the key and placed it in a cubbyhole inside the desk.

"I hope you've enjoyed your stay," she said.

"It was everything I expected it to be," Mr. Miller said. He clutched his briefcase close to his side. His monotone voice left Molly at a loss for a response.

"Well, then, that's good," Molly said, finally. *I think*, she added to herself.

"Thank you," Mr. Miller said. "I'll be going now."

Molly watched him walk to the front door and step onto the front porch. As he turned around to pull the door closed, she was almost certain she saw him smile. *Strange little man*, she thought to herself, not for the first time. She reached for her purse, put on her jacket and left thoughts of Mr. Miller behind as she headed into town to run errands.

CHAPTER THIRTY-ONE

Susie rummaged through the bookshelves in the library. Time was running out. Molly could be back from afternoon errands soon. Dan could get bored and come looking for her. Luckily, Sadie had dragged Bryce into town to check out Eleanor's. And thank heavens that weird guest Mr. Miller was already gone. He gave her the creeps, though she'd never been able to put her finger on exactly why. Probably one of those past life things, she thought. If a person believed in all that malarkey.

She'd been through five rows already, removing each book, shaking it out and replacing it on the shelf. Three rows remained, all of them high above the floor. It made more sense that the money would be hidden on a top shelf, but she'd taken a shot at the lower ones first. For one thing, the most obvious hiding place was often the least likely. For another, she was too short to reach the upper shelves.

Failing to find anything within the lower rows, she poked around the office and kitchen areas, finally locating a three-tiered step stool. She carried it to the library, locked the door and started in on the upper shelves.

Thirty minutes later, she was convinced the library was a dead end. The shelves held books and nothing else. She checked underneath a throw rug, behind picture frames, and inside an antique china cabinet. No hidden compartments, no trap doors.

Susie rolled the rug back down and opened the library back up. Taking the step stool back to the kitchen, she weighed her options. She'd already checked the downstairs guest rooms, though they'd never been a serious consideration. Hiding anything in a room where strangers would come and go made no sense. Even the library was a long shot. But it had deserved a chance just because of the sheer number of possibilities.

She tried to put herself in Molly's place to figure out where she might have hidden the money. It was a long stretch for a clever sleuth-slash-criminal to get into the mindset of a plain office girl who took advantage of a fluke opportunity. What kind of mind would be capable of switching gears so quickly, aside from hers, of course? Ah, there it was. They had more in common than physical size.

Susie had a sudden, sickening thought. Was it possible that Molly had been in on it from the start? That would mean that Al had set her up. No, after all the years she'd worked for him, she couldn't believe he'd do that. She was too valuable to him for future work. And, from everything she'd seen of Molly, the girl just didn't have it in her. How it was that she'd caught Bryce's attention was beyond comprehension.

The wave of bitterness that accompanied that thought filled her with renewed energy. She made a quick pass through the inside of the inn again. Wherever Molly had hidden the money, it wasn't inside.

Susie slipped out the front door and down the pathway to the Cottage Suite. Cracking the door open, she heard Dan's snoring before she even stepped inside the room. She pulled the door closed and looked through the back garden.

Unless she wanted to start digging up the ground, there was no place to search.

She circled around the back corner of the building and checked the electrical box. That was pointless, she realized as she shut the cover. No one would hide money where a meter reader would find it. Moving along, she rolled a large potted container to the side, checking for a recessed area beneath it, but to no avail. Two additional potted arrangements yielded the same thing: nothing.

Which is when she came to the metal tool shed, halfway between the front and rear yards. The tiny, nondescript side yard was so insignificant that she had missed it completely.

Glancing around, she reassured herself she was alone. Shrubbery blocked the view from outside the property, and the shed was too low to be seen from inside the inn. And the shed was small. She'd be able to search it quickly and still have time to freshen up before the wine and cheese hour.

She wasted no time pulling the latch to the side and opening both doors. Inside the shed, two rows of wooden planks held garden tools, while bags of fertilizer and potting soil lined the floor. A shovel, rake and hoe leaned against the right hand corner. A spray bottle for water hung from a hook inside one of the doors. It was a ridiculous place to hide money, which made it a perfect place.

Susie ran her hands along the top shelf, shifting tools from side to side, but found nothing below or behind them. The lower shelf yielded the same result. Flattening her palms under the shelf, the wood was smooth to the right and center, but her hand struck a lump of tape, to the left. She fiddled around the tape with her fingers until it peeled back. Her hopes soared as she felt a metal object beneath her fingertips, thinking it might be a key to a safe. But those thoughts deflated just as quickly when she pulled it out and found it was a common house key. Of course Molly would have a spare key hidden. She was just that sort of obnoxious, organized personality.

Susie replaced the key, attempting to press the tape against it securely, but it didn't hold. The key tumbled and fell behind the bags of fertilizer. Frustrated, Susie reached down to retrieve it and froze. The key balanced on the handle of a box. Gardening tools, perhaps? Seed packets? Or could it finally be what she was searching for?

She retrieved the key, placed it on top of the lower shelf and lifted the box out from behind the bag. Setting it on the ground, she paused before opening it. If it contained nothing but miscellaneous supplies, she'd wasted more time. The entire trip could even have been pointless, worse than pointless, really, considering she'd had to deal with Dan all weekend.

The plastic slide latch was easy to pull aside. Not even a lock on the box, Susie mused. How foolish. Even worse, it was discouraging. The likelihood of money being hidden, but not locked up, was slim. But as she lifted the lid and inspected the interior of the box, she gasped. Bundles of hundred dollar bills were carefully stacked side-by-side below an empty, upper tray. She had been right all along. Molly was the thief.

Susie needed to think quickly. She could try to move it to the car while Dan was still napping. No, that wouldn't be smart. Anyone could see her walking to the street. Besides, she needed to take advantage of finding the money at Molly's, as she had planned all along. Once Molly was found with the money, the case would be solved and she could shop to her heart's content with the rather large portion that wouldn't be recovered. Not only would Al be off her back, but Molly would get what she deserved.

Playing it safe was the best bet. She latched the lid on the box, replaced it behind the bag and scanned the interior of the tool shed. Everything looked the same as when she first entered it. Leaving the stash, she closed up the shed and returned to the barn suite. She'd return later to siphon off her share.

CHAPTER THIRTY-TWO

Sadie sat across from Bryce at Eleanor's, reading the daily lunch specials. Seven days of the week, seven different specials. All looked delicious, as did everything on the regular menu.

"Ah, the Southwestern Salad, that's it for me," Sadie said, setting the menu on the edge of the table. "Chopped lettuce, black beans, diced tomatoes, avocado, corn, tortilla strips and cheddar cheese. Can't go wrong with that combination. Makes me want to head back to Santa Fe. Always loved the food there. Just might make that my next trip."

Bryce set his menu on top of hers. "The French Dip is tempting, but I'm going with Eleanor's Rueben, since you recommended it so highly."

"Room for one more?"

"Eleanor, so glad you're here!" Sadie said. She motioned for the café owner to join them. "This is Bryce; he's staying at Cranberry Cottage, too. I was hoping you two might meet."

"Glad to meet you, Bryce," Eleanor said, taking the offered seat. "How do you like our quaint town?"

"It's full of little surprises," Bryce said, smiling.

"Yes, indeed," Sadie beamed. "You never know what you might find in a small town. Like this gentleman right here, for example, who is...working on a novel, isn't that right?" Sadie gestured toward Bryce, who simply nodded.

"Is that so?" Eleanor smiled. "I've thought about writing a book myself, though it would be a cookbook. My friends keep bugging me to put one together."

"Well, I'm not surprised, with everything I've been hearing about this place. I'm glad Sadie finally dragged me here." Bryce paused as a server stopped by and took their order.

"Good choices, both of you," Eleanor said. "That salad is delicious with the cilantro-lime dressing and the Reuben is a local favorite." She paused, seeing the restaurant hostess signaling to her from the front. "Excuse me a moment. That must be Casey," she said as she stood up and headed to the front of the restaurant.

"Who is Casey?" Bryce leaned back in his chair, paying only minor attention to his question.

"Eleanor's husband," Sadie answered. "He owns the local hardware store. Nice man. He's probably picking up food to go. I think she makes him a lunch every day that he can take back to work."

"A good wife." Bryce smiled. "And an advantage of having a restaurant in the family, within walking distance, no less."

The conversation paused as their meals arrived. Bryce's eyes widened as he took in the hefty sandwich and accompanying fries. He grinned and nodded his head in approval. Sadie wasted no time pouring dressing over her salad and spearing the fresh greens with her fork. Bryce followed suit and took a bite of his sandwich.

Eleanor returned to the table, taking a seat and smiling. "I see you're enjoying your meals."

"How could we not, Eleanor?" Sadie said, stabbing another forkful of salad. "Everything here is addictive. Obviously your husband thinks so. I see you're still fixing his lunches."

"Of course I am," Eleanor said. "He works hard. We both do. Anything we can do to help each other out, we do. It's convenient we have the restaurant. He doesn't have to close up to get something to eat, yet he gets a chance to get away for a few minutes when he picks up lunch."

"And you get to see him midday, as well," Sadie pointed out. She poured extra dressing on the salad with a flourish.

"Not normally," Eleanor said. "He usually picks it up at the hostess stand on his own. I make sure it's ready ahead of time, in case we're busy."

"But today?" Sadie said.

"Sometimes when Casey sees that it isn't too busy, he'll have the hostess get my attention, and he'll tell me little stories about his customers. He wanted to share a strange encounter he had," Eleanor said.

Bryce's eyebrows lifted. "Strange? In a bad way?"

Eleanor shook her head. "No, not in a bad way. Just weird. A man came into the store, browsing the aisles slowly. Bought a couple of tackle boxes."

"How is that weird?" Sadie asked. "You must have fishing in this area. There's a whole ocean just down the street."

"Casey said he didn't seem like the fisherman type," Eleanor said.

"Maybe they were a gift?" Bryce took another bite of the Reuben, turning it sideways to keep sauerkraut from spilling out.

"Maybe," Eleanor said. "Casey just thought he was a bit odd. Must have been a guest somewhere, said he was checking out soon."

Sadie and Bryce exchanged glances.

"What did he look like?" Sadie set her fork down and took a sip of iced tea.

Eleanor shrugged her shoulders. "Short, glasses, not very friendly, almost rude – that's how Casey described him."

"Sounds like one of the guests at Cranberry Cottage," Sadie said. "A Mr. Miller. Quiet, keeps to himself. I saw him loading his car when I walked over here, so he must have been getting ready to check out."

"It's not a big deal," Eleanor said, standing up. "He just gave Casey the creeps. Anyway, I'll let you finish your meal in peace. I need to see how dinner prep is going." She pushed in her chair and returned to the kitchen.

"What do you think?" Bryce asked Sadie as he pushed his plate away in surrender.

"Nothing, really," Sadie said. "He's a strange man, but I don't think buying tackle boxes is that weird. Maybe he's planning to take a couple of sons on a fishing trip in the future?"

"Sons?" Sadie laughed. "There's nothing about that man that says 'married' to me."

"Nephews, then," Bryce proposed. "Or maybe he goes fishing by himself and likes to be overly prepared."

Sadie agreed. "He does seem that type, a bit on the obsessive side." She set down her fork and moved her salad plate to the side of the table.

"Now, about Molly," Sadie continued.

The server removed the plates from the table, took them to the kitchen and returned with two small scoops of cranberry sorbet, each in a miniature crock and matching saucer.

"Homemade, compliments of Eleanor," the server said, setting a check for the rest of the meal on the table.

"Oh, my, what a delightful surprise! Tell her thank you!" Sadie wasted no time digging in.

"So, back to Molly," Bryce said after the server walked away. Sadie caught the softness in his voice.

"You're smitten," Sadie grinned.

"Smitten – what an old-fashioned word, Sadie." Bryce tasted the sorbet, raising his eyebrows in approval.

"Now, now, young man," Sadie said. "I'm old and I'm fashioned, but I'd hardly say I'm old fashioned."

Bryce laughed. "You've got me there. But, you're right. I suppose I'm 'smitten,' as you say. Beyond that, I'm convinced she had nothing to do with the bank robbery, not before, not after. Still, we have no way to prove it. I'm running out of time to report back to *Binky* and we haven't identified another suspect *or* found any money."

Sadie smiled; she hadn't missed Bryce's exaggerated use of her first husband's nickname. "What do you suggest?" She slipped a final spoonful of sorbet into her mouth.

"Finding both would be nice."

"Yes, it would. But, whatever happens, don't worry about *Binky*," Sadie agreed, imitating Bryce's exaggeration of the name. "He trusts my judgment, plus I have decades of experience getting him to back off. If I say she's not guilty, he'll believe me."

Both stood. "My treat," Bryce said, leaving a couple of crisp bills alongside the check. Sadie waved a thank you to Eleanor, who was talking with another customer.

Bryce held the front door open as they stepped outside. "I'm heading back to the inn to pretend to work on the book I'm not writing. I'll walk back with you."

"I have a few stops to make first," Sadie said.

"Let me guess…shopping?" Bryce laughed.

"What else? That and I'd like to drop into Casey's for a minute," Sadie said. "I'll catch up with you in a bit."

CHAPTER THIRTY-THREE

The barn suite was empty when Susie stepped in, which was a relief. It was about time that good-for-nothing fake husband of hers stopped being lazy. Hopefully he'd gone into town to buy her something. It was one advantage of the sickening crush he maintained – trinkets he'd pick up as attempts to draw her closer. As if that were even possible! But she had mentioned some earrings at one Cranberry Cove shop that she hadn't been able to lift the day before. He'd probably gone back to get them for her. She smiled. At least there were some perks to having him around.

She took advantage of having the suite to herself, running a hot bath in the Jacuzzi tub and adding lavender bath oils that the inn provided. Slipping out of her clothing, she slid into the fragrant water. The leisurely soak relaxed her and, for a moment, she almost felt she was on vacation. She could get used to living like this – aside from the dinky town and having to put up with Dan. Pulling a fashion magazine from a bath-side table, she flipped through the pages, pausing to admire a full-page jewelry ad. Emerald earrings, gold bangles with channel set diamonds, and a dangling pendant with a pearl drop ruby – all perfectly sized to fit in a pocket. How delightful! Magazine shoplifting was almost as fun as the real thing.

She set the magazine aside, stepped out of the bath and toweled off. Deciding against a cream colored sweater and matching slacks – after all, the tool shed wasn't exactly pristine – she pulled on a pair of rhinestone-studded jeans and a black designer sweatshirt, hesitating over her favorite heels. Flats were more suitable for this task. She slipped into a brown pair that wouldn't show dirt easily.

Her suitcase was always packed full when she traveled. Better to be over-prepared than under, she figured. And this time the excess had made it easy to carry extra make-up bags, the kind that could be purchased at any drug store. The ones she'd brought along featured prints that she could barely tolerate, but they'd serve their purpose. Had Dan noticed them, he would have simply thought they were for her expanding jewelry collection. She pulled two from the suitcase, tucked them under one arm and headed out.

The tool shed looked exactly as she'd left it an hour before, the latch tightly pressed against the wooden doors. She glanced in each direction. She'd have to work quickly, but it wouldn't take long to fill the cosmetic bags. She needed to leave enough to make sure Molly was caught, but she could take most of it. After all, any amateur thief would have spent a good part of it by now. It was just one more reason that Molly deserved to be caught. That never should have been Molly's money to begin with.

Susie pulled the latch aside and opened the tool shed. It was all coming together now, finally. All the mix-ups, all the role-playing, and all the patience it had taken to deal with Dan. These hassles would be over for good. Just a few more steps and she could solve the case, turn enough of the money in to cover her tracks and be done with the whole disaster.

Bending down to retrieve the box, she gasped. No, it wasn't possible! The space behind the bag of potting soil had been well hidden when she'd left, yet was empty. Frantic, she pulled each bag away from the shed's back wall, wondering if she'd confused the location. It was no use. The box with the money was gone.

Panicked, she shoved the bags back into the shed. Had Molly caught on? Had she seen Susie discover the box and then moved the money to a different hiding place? There was no way she was going to let that opportunistic office girl get away with the money. She slammed the door, not bothering to latch it. Furious, she stormed back to the barn suite.

CHAPTER THIRTY-FOUR

Dan was seated on the couch when Susie flew through the door. He jumped up and turned toward her with a grin, but pulled back at the sight of her furious expression.

"What's wrong?" Dan said.

Susie crossed the room, did an about-face and crossed again, beating her fist against her forehead as she paced. Dan frowned. She only exhibited this gesture under extreme stress. He remained quiet. Some kind of tantrum was bound to follow.

Susie wracked her brain, trying to think of a way to explain the situation without giving herself away. She'd tagged along with him to Cranberry Cove on the pretense of catching Molly. She might as well keep playing that story line. If nothing else, it would buy her more time to track the money down.

"I...," Susie started, trying to settle down enough to keep her story straight. "I'm just frustrated. I was sure I'd...stumbled upon proof that Molly was guilty, but I was wrong. You know I hate being wrong."

She threw herself down on the couch, buried her head in her hands and took a deep breath. Maybe he would go fetch a glass of wine if the inn had it out already. She grabbed her cell phone and checked the time. Damn, she thought. Another twenty minutes. She could use a generous goblet of Pinot Noir right then – or two or three, for that matter.

"It's OK," Dan said. "I was going to say…"

Susie snapped her head up and cut him off.

"Don't patronize me," she shouted, then lowered her voice quickly. Things were bad enough without blowing their newlywed cover. She needed to keep her temper under control. "It's not OK."

"But it *is* OK," Dan repeated, a huge grin plastered across his face. "That's what I'm trying to tell you! I've solved the case!"

A dread filled Susie's gut.

"What do you mean, you solved the case?" she said.

Dan looked like he was about to burst with pride. The knot in Susie's mid-region tightened. He dropped to his knees in front of her, so they were at eye level. For the first time, the thought that he was about to propose was not her worst fear.

"I found the money!" Dan whispered. He looked over his shoulder, a gesture Susie found ridiculous in their private suite.

"You found *what*?" Susie tried to juggle the thoughts that hit at the same time: How had he found it? Where was it now? How could she portion some off before they turned it in? Had he counted it?

"I found the money," Dan repeated. "That was the evidence we needed to turn Molly in. Don't you see? This is a big score for us – the prestige, not to mention the reward money."

Maybe a big score for you, Susie thought to herself. That reward was peanuts compared to what she planned to get. She mulled over a course of action, hoping to steer Dan in a direction that would work in her favor.

"OK," she said. "Let's figure out a plan. Where did you put the money?"

Dan stood up, looking puzzled. "Don't you want to know where I found it?"

"Of course I do!" Susie was sure her voice was overly enthusiastic. Forgetting to ask where he found it was a careless slip. A calmer partner would have caught that. She needed to keep in control or she'd blow the whole deal.

"You won't believe it," Dan said. "It was in a shed around the far side of the building. I was trying to find a replacement bulb for that pathway light. She had it stored in a toolbox, of all things! Or maybe it was a tackle box. It did look like my Uncle Jim's box that he takes on fishing trips, come to think of it."

"Wow, she hid it in a tool shed!" Susie forced herself to speak slowly. "Go figure." She shook her head, counted to three and returned to her previous question.

"OK, so where did you put it? We need to make sure it's safe until we turn it in."

Susie waited for an answer, but Dan just grinned. The knot in her stomach began to twist again.

"Oh, you don't have to worry about it being safe," Dan said. "I went directly to the police and turned it in."

"You did WHAT?" Susie shouted, jumping up and grabbing Dan's shirt with her fists. "You are such an imbecile! What am I going to tell Al?"

Dan pulled back and stared at her, eyes wide.

"What is the matter with you?" he said. "Of course I turned it in to the police. What else would I do with it? That's the whole reason we came here – to find the money, turn it in and prove the innkeeper is guilty! And…who's Al?"

Susie let go of Dan's shirt, thrusting him backward as she stormed out of the suite. She headed directly for the kitchen of the inn, bursting in through the side door. Molly whirled around in shock as Susie flew across the room, her finger pointed in Molly's face. Slices of cheese slid off a plate that Molly was holding and fell on the floor.

"You!" she hissed. "You thought you'd get away with this!"

"What are you talking about?" Molly stammered.

"You know perfectly well what I'm talking about," Susie said. "You should have stayed down when I told you to. That was my job, not yours! Did Al put you up to this to begin with? Having me follow your schedule, match your outfit, go to the window next to yours…I can't believe he did this to me, after all I've done for him – and *YOU*, an amateur!"

"What?" Molly's face turned pale as the pieces came together. She looked over Susie's shoulder, causing Susie to spin around.

"Really, *Susie*," Bryce said from the back kitchen table, his voice calm. "And *YOU*, a pro, losing your cool like this. Not something Sonja would do."

Susie gasped, one hand flying up to cover her mouth.

"Now, now, temper, temper. That's a fatal flaw in our business, my dear. You should know better," Bryce said.

"Who's Sonja?" Molly said.

Dan burst through the side door, repeating his question from the barn suite conversation.

"Who's Al?" he said.

"Sonja will explain, Dan," Bryce said.

Dan turned toward the table, seeing Bryce for the first time since entering the kitchen.

"Who's Sonja?" Dan said.

"Your fake wife," Bryce answered.

"What? *Susie* is my fake wife," Dan shouted. "Er…I mean, my wife."

"Fake wife?" Molly said. "I thought you guys were newlyweds."

"Shut up," Susie shouted at Molly. "In fact, all of you shut up. I'm done with this whole fiasco."

Susie headed for the side door, but Dan blocked her exit.

"You owe me an explanation."

"I don't owe you anything. It's enough I've had to put up with you," Susie countered. "All I want now is to get out of this stupid excuse for a town." Turning, she aimed for the main kitchen door, but stopped as two police officers stepped into the room.

"I don't think that's going to happen," the first officer said.

"At least not until we get you extradited back to Tallahassee," the other added. He removed his police cap with one hand and reached for his handcuffs with the other.

"Did I miss anything?" Sadie said, entering the kitchen, both arms overloaded with shopping bags. She gave Bryce a knowing smile.

Susie ignored Sadie and shouted at the police. "What about her?" she said, nodding toward Molly. She struggled against being handcuffed. "She's the one who had the money in her tool shed! Why aren't you taking *her* in?"

"What money in the tool shed?" Molly said. "There's no money in the tool shed."

"Not now there isn't," Dan said to Molly. "But only because we found it and turned it in to the police. But, wait…if you didn't put it in there, who did?"

"That's a good question," the first officer said, turning to the second, who had just finished handcuffing Susie. "Maybe we'd better take Molly in, too."

"I don't think that will be necessary," Sadie interrupted. "Molly, there's someone here to see you."

"She's a little busy now, don't you think?" Susie snapped.

"Bring him in," Bryce said. "Sadie knows what she's doing. Besides, it can't get much more confusing than it already is. Or entertaining, for that matter."

Sadie gestured through the kitchen door. A minute later Casey stood in the doorway, holding a piece of paper.

"I hate to barge in, but Sadie insisted I come over," the owner of the hardware store said. His eyes grew wide as he looked around and took in the wild scene. Susie was as red as a bicycle reflector, Molly, pale as white kitchen tile and the rest of the room's occupants wore expressions as assorted as a box of miscellaneous faucet washers.

"Casey?" Molly said, "I didn't order supplies this week."

"I know," Casey said. "I'm not here to deliver anything. I just wanted to see if the guy who won this week's raffle was here. Sadie thought he might be here, but I don't see him."

He glanced around the room. Shoulders shrugged and heads shook from side to side.

"No one cares about a stupid raffle right now," Susie spit out.

"I think you might when you hear what Casey here has to say," Sadie said. She winked at Bryce, a gesture that no one in the room seemed to understand.

"Sorry to interrupt, Molly," Casey said, ignoring Susie's previous remark. "The guy just said he was checking out and I was hoping to catch him before he left town. He won twenty bucks."

"Wow, twenty bucks," Susie said, her tone laced with sarcasm. "I wouldn't want to miss out on that windfall."

"No need to be snide, my dear." Bryce said. "It goes without saying that Sonja never would have bothered with such a measly sum." Susie glared.

"Who is Sonja?" Sadie said.

"Hold on, Casey." One police officer stopped him as he was turning to leave. "What did the guy buy – the one who won the raffle and said he was checking out?"

"It was a tackle box," Casey said, looking down at the receipt. "Actually, two tackle boxes, to be specific."

"This gentleman turned in a tackle box filled with the money," the officer said to his partner, indicating Dan with a nod of his head.

The kitchen grew silent. Dan was the first to break the lull in conversation.

"Well, what do you know," Dan said. "An honest person found the money and...wait, why would he bring it here?"

Susie burst out laughing. "Dan, you are such an idiot!" She tried unsuccessfully to bring a handcuffed arm around and then exhaled upward to blow her bangs out of her eyes.

Molly looked at Bryce. "I don't understand either."

"I think I can explain," Bryce said. "Mr. Miller took the money from Susie after she robbed the bank."

"That was never part of the plan!" Susie said before turning to Molly. "Besides, aren't you the one who crashed into me?"

"I didn't crash into anyone," Molly said.

"What plan?" Dan looked at Susie. Getting no response, he turned to Molly, who shrugged in return.

"Maybe it was an impulse – an opportunity, right place and right time. And he changed his mind later. Or maybe it was an accident," Bryce continued. "It doesn't matter. He didn't come here to return it out of the kindness of his heart. He came here to plant it and pin the blame on Molly, since she was a suspect already. He may have even thought she was the one who took it originally. That was what the news coverage made it look like."

"Well, it looks pretty clear who the thief is," the first officer said, turning his attention back to Susie. "Let's go."

"Wait, before you take her, I just have to ask," Bryce said, facing Susie. "What really happened to that Van Gogh in Austria?"

"As if I'm going to tell you!" Susie exclaimed.

"And those emeralds we weren't able to retrieve in Barcelona? I don't suppose you know anything about them, either?" Bryce crossed his arms.

"You'll never know!" Susie shouted over her shoulder as the first officer pulled her through the door.

"Who *ARE* you people?" the second policeman said, shaking his head. He put his uniform cap back on and followed his partner out the door.

Molly and Dan exchanged confused looks. Bryce grinned and gave a thumb's up in Sadie's direction. Sadie looked around the room and lifted both arms, palms up, shopping bags dangling, as she spoke.

"Wine and cheese, anyone?"

CHAPTER THIRTY-FIVE

Moonlight cast a glow across the Pacific Ocean, sparkling like stars on a clear winter's night. The restaurant's expansive picture window offered a magical view as Molly and Bryce settled in against plush cushions. A flickering candle in the center of their ocean view booth sent shadows of dancing flames across the white linen tablecloth. A petite vase held a single rose with sprigs of greenery. Outside, floodlights illuminated the crashing waves below while nostalgic piano bar melodies floated in from the cocktail lounge.

"I don't know if I'll ever understand this completely," Molly said. She thanked the restaurant's host as he placed two menus on the table before walking away.

"Sometimes not understanding is best," Bryce said. "Don't you think you've been through enough? Now that the other guests have headed home - Sadie to San Francisco, and Dan to St. Louis - the inn is quiet. You can let the stress go and breathe. Leave it behind you as an unfortunate misunderstanding."

"An unfortunate misunderstanding? That may be the biggest understatement I've ever heard." Molly laughed then became serious. "Wait, I thought Dan and Susie were from Boston. Did *everyone* here register with false addresses and fake stories?"

"Not Sadie," Bryce said. "She's really from San Francisco and does have a boutique called Flair."

Molly sighed. "Thank goodness! At least one person came here without some kind of cover story!"

Bryce smiled, but said nothing.

"What about this mysterious 'bad guy' you referred to before, the one who hired you to bring me back to Tallahassee?"

Bryce acknowledged the question with a slight nod of his head. "I never should have mentioned him. It only upset you and wasn't something you could do anything about. But I needed you to listen to me. As it turns out, you don't need to be worried about him."

"Really? Are you sure?" Molly frowned, thinking back over their initial conversations. "You seemed convinced I was in danger."

"And I believe that was true at the time. But you aren't anymore."

"Just like that?" Molly asked.

"Not quite 'just like that,' as you say," Bryce replied. "But, for one thing, the police have the money, so it's not going anywhere except back to the bank."

"And the other thing?"

Bryce smiled. "Let's just say he's dropping the matter as a favor to an old friend, someone he was fond of long ago. It's also clear now that you had nothing to do with the robbery."

Molly leaned back against the soft padding of the booth and sighed. "Well, it's about time someone figured that out!"

Bryce nodded toward Molly's menu. "So, what looks good to you?"

"Anything without cranberries." Bryce laughed and Molly grinned back.

"The pine-nut encrusted halibut looks great. With the roasted wild mushroom soup to start."

"Sounds perfect," Molly said. "I'll have the same thing."

"And champagne," Bryce added just before the server left the table. "And we'll order something decadent to share afterward."

Molly smiled. A sweet dessert and two spoons could be the perfect way to turn an already pleasant meal at Ocean into a romantic dinner. She set her menu aside as the melody of "Begin the Beguine" floated in from the bar.

"I love these old tunes from the thirties and forties." Molly closed her eyes and listened to the blended sound of piano music and ocean waves. "They're so soothing."

"It's good to see you relaxed," Bryce said, reaching for Molly's hand.

"Maybe it's because I'm not looking over my shoulder anymore."

"I'm sure that's part of it," Bryce said. "But I hope it's not the only reason."

Molly had a good mind to tease him by ignoring his comment, just to keep his ego under control. But he was right. Having him around had soothed her nerves. It felt reassuring to know someone believed in her.

"You've helped so much," she said. "I don't know what would have happened if you hadn't been here. I might have been headed for free room and board, just like Susie is now."

"And she'd be free," Bryce said. "Undoubtedly, off on another adventure."

"Like in Austria and Barcelona?" Molly suggested, a secondary question hidden within the spoken words. Even in the confusion of the kitchen interaction with the police, Molly hadn't missed the obvious reference to Bryce and Susie… or was it Sonja ... having worked together before.

"Perhaps," Bryce said, reaching across the table to squeeze Molly's hand. "We all have pasts. I was a private investigator working with a double-crossing thief. And you, my dear, were a wanted bank robber."

Molly laughed. "Yes, I suppose that's true, for a little while, anyway."

Conversation paused as the server returned with champagne. After he popped it open, he set the bottle in an ice bucket alongside the table and left.

"So, if Susie had found the money that Mr. Miller planted, she would have taken it," Molly continued. "Then I wouldn't have been accused in the end."

"Yes and no," Bryce said. "I'm sure she would have taken most of it, but she would have left enough to turn you in and leave herself in the clear. That would be a perfect plan, from her point of view. She'd get the money and you'd get the blame. She'd split the reward with Dan. And don't forget, she thought you were the one who took it from her in the first place."

"Mr. Miller also thought I'd taken it or he never would have come out here." Molly took a sip of champagne, nodding at Bryce to do the same.

"Only because he followed the news," Bryce said. "Some people believe everything on the news is true."

"But it didn't matter to him, one way or another," Bryce continued. "He just wanted to get rid of it."

"Everyone thought I'd taken it," Molly mused.

"I didn't, not once I'd met you," Bryce said.

"But you did think I was guilty at first," Molly pointed out. "Or you wouldn't have come here, either."

"And it's a good thing I thought so or I never would have met you."

"Yes, though I never dreamed being falsely accused of a crime could be a good thing." Molly shook her head and looked out the window. Seagulls circled and landed at the water's edge, white specks against the dark, wet sand.

"What will you do now that this case is solved?" Molly said tentatively, turning her head back to Bryce.

"I'm not sure. Maybe I really will write a novel. Chasing criminals around the world has given me a few good plot ideas." Bryce grinned as he reached for the champagne bottle.

"I imagine so," Molly laughed.

"And, now that your life is your own again, will you go back to Tallahassee?" Bryce topped off Molly's glass with champagne before doing the same to his own. He replaced the bottle in the ice bucket.

"No," Molly said. "There was never much for me there. I like Cranberry Cove and running Cranberry Cottage Bed and Breakfast suits me. It's what Aunt Maggie would want me to do. And I was ready for a change in spite of the drama it took to get me here. I've needed a new start."

"Well, I think you found one. In fact, maybe we both did." Bryce lifted his champagne to toast. "Here's to new beginnings."

Molly met it with her own glass.

EPILOGUE

Mr. Miller sat back in his folding chair and looked out at the river. The sound of the water tumbling over rocks soothed him. Solitude was all he'd ever wanted. Now it was his. No people, the nearest town fifty miles away.

He reached out with his arm and grabbed a fly from the tackle box, attached it to the fishing line and cast out. As was his habit, he made sure his hands were dry. There was no use risking water getting into the lower compartment.

He was pleased with how efficiently his plot had succeeded - right down to the ten thousand dollar reward he was due. The bank would have the rest of the money back soon, thanks to his anonymous phone call to the police. He clucked his tongue as he thought of the perfect, succinct wording in the resignation letter he'd mailed on the way out of Cranberry Cove:

Dear Supervisor,

Please accept my resignation, effective immediately.

Regards,

Charles Henry Miller, III

He latched the box and set it aside. The future was all he looked at now. A serene future with an upper tray of flies, sorted into groups of twenty and a lower tray of bills, sorted into groups of thousands.

AUNT MAGGIE'S CRANBERRY COTTAGE COOKBOOK

Cranberry Scones
Cranberry Pancakes
Cranberry Applesauce
Cranberry Nut Bread
Cranberry Lemon Muffins
Cranberry Pumpkin Muffins
Cranberry Swirl Coffee Cake
Cranberry White Chocolate Bars
Cranberry Relish
Cranberry Brie Bites
Cranberry Kale Salad w/ Quinoa
Cranberry Wild Rice Soup
Cranberry Cornbread
Cranberry Pear Walnut Cobbler
Cranberry Citrus Sorbet

Cranberry Scones

Ingredients:

1 cup all-purpose flour
1/4 cup sugar
1-1/2 teaspoons baking powder
1/8 teaspoon salt
1/4 cup cold butter
4 tablespoons milk
1 egg, beaten
1/4 cup dried cranberries
1/4 teaspoon coarse sugar

Directions:

In a small bowl, combine the flour, sugar, baking powder and salt.
Cut in butter until mixture resembles coarse crumbs.
In a small bowl, combine milk and 2 tablespoons beaten egg; add to crumb mixture just until moistened.
Stir in cranberries.
Turn onto a floured surface; knead gently 6-8 times. Pat into a 6-in. circle.
Cut into six wedges. Separate and place on a greased baking sheet.
Brush with remaining egg; sprinkle with coarse sugar.
Bake at 425° for approx. 12 minutes or until golden brown. Serve warm.

Cranberry Pancakes

Ingredients:

¾ cup milk
2 tablespoons melted butter
1 egg
1 cup flour
2 teaspoons baking powder
2 tablespoons sugar
1/2 teaspoon salt
1/2 cup fresh or frozen cranberries
1 teaspoon sugar (for cranberries)

Directions:

Beat milk, melted butter, and egg together in a bowl.
Mix flour, baking powder, 2 tablespoons sugar, and salt together in a separate bowl and add to wet ingredients mixing just enough to wet the flour.
Cut cranberries in half. Place in microwave safe bowl and sprinkle in the 1 tsp of sugar. Microwave on high and stir every 15 seconds till cranberries start to bubble. Let cool and add to pancake mixture.
Preheat griddle with a pat of butter till water droplets dance on the surface.
Pour cranberry batter on griddle. Cook till surface bubbles. Flip and cook other side.

Cranberry Applesauce

Ingredients:

4 large cooking apples, peeled, cored and cut into chunks
1/2 cup fresh or frozen cranberries
1/4 cup sugar
1/2 cup water
1/8 teaspoon ground nutmeg
1/4 teaspoon ground cinnamon

Directions:

Mix all ingredients in a saucepan and bring to a boil.
Cover and cook over low heat until the cranberries pop and the apples are soft (15-20 minutes).
Place in a food processor and blend until smooth.
Serve warm or chilled.

Cranberry Nut Bread

Ingredients:

2 cups flour
1 cups granulated sugar
1/2 teaspoon salt
1/2 teaspoon baking soda
1 1/2 teaspoon baking powder
1 egg, slightly beaten
1/2 cup orange juice
1/8 cup hot water
1/8 cup melted butter
1/2 tablespoon grated orange rind
1 cup chopped fresh (or frozen) cranberries
1/2 cup chopped nuts

Directions:

Preheat oven to 350°F.
Combine all dry ingredients in a large bowl.
Mix eggs, orange juice, hot water, butter and orange rind; stir into flour mix.
Fold in cranberries and nuts.
Spoon the batter into a greased loaf pan.
Bake for 1 hour and 10 minutes or until a toothpick inserted in the center comes out clean.
Remove from pan and cool on a wire rack.

Cranberry Lemon Muffins

Ingredients:

1/2 cup plain yogurt
1 cup sugar
3 large eggs
1 tablespoon lemon zest
1/2 teaspoon vanilla extract
1/2 cup canola oil
1 1/2 cups all purpose flour
2 teaspoons baking powder
2 cups fresh whole cranberries (do not cut in half)

Directions:

Preheat oven to 350°F.
Grease muffin tin or line with paper liners.
In a large bowl, beat together yogurt, sugar, and eggs.
Add lemon zest and vanilla extract.
Stir in oil.
In a medium bowl, stir together flour and baking powder.
Gently fold flour mixture into wet ingredients. Stir until just moistened.
Stir in cranberries.
Spoon the batter into muffin tin. Bake for 20-25 minutes.
Cool on a wire rack.

Cranberry Pumpkin Muffins

Ingredients:

2 cups all-purpose flour
3/4 cup sugar
3 teaspoons baking powder
1 teaspoon ground cinnamon
1/4 teaspoon ground nutmeg
1/4 teaspoon salt
1 cup canned pumpkin
1/2 cup canola oil
2 eggs
1 cup dried cranberries

Directions:

Preheat oven to 400°F.
Grease 12 regular-sized muffin cups.
Mix together flour, sugar, baking powder, cinnamon, nutmeg, and salt.
Stir in pumpkin, oil, eggs and cranberries. Do not over mix.
Divide batter evenly among 12 muffin cups.
Bake 20-25 minutes or until a toothpick inserted in the center comes out clean.
Cool on a wire rack.

Cranberry Swirl Coffee Cake

Ingredients:

1 stick butter
1 cup sugar
2 eggs
1 teaspoon baking powder
1 teaspoon baking soda
2 cups flour
1/2 teaspoon salt
1/2 pint sour cream
1 teaspoon almond extract
7 0z can whole cranberry sauce
1/2 cup chopped walnuts

Directions:

Preheat oven to 350°F.
Cream butter and sugar together.
Add unbeaten eggs one at a time, using mixer at med speed.
Sift together dry ingredients.
Reduce speed and add dry ingredients, alternating with sour cream.
Add almond extract.
Pour a layer of batter in the bottom of a greased tube pan.
Add a layer of swirled cranberry sauce. Repeat layers.
Sprinkle with nuts and bake for approx. 55 min.

Cranberry White Chocolate Bars

Ingredients:

2 large eggs
½ teaspoon vanilla extract
1 cup sugar
1 cup all-purpose flour
¼ teaspoon salt
½ cup butter, melted
3/4 cups fresh or frozen (thawed) cranberries, coarsely chopped
1/2 (11-oz) bag white chocolate chips

Directions:

Preheat oven to 350°F.
Whisk together eggs and vanilla extract in a mixing bowl until blended.
Gradually add sugar, beating until blended.
Stir in flour, salt and melted butter.
Gently stir in cranberries and white chocolate chips.
Spread dough in a lightly greased 8-inch square pan.
Bake 38 to 40 minutes or until a toothpick inserted in center comes out clean.
Cool and cut into bars.

Cranberry Relish

Ingredients:

1 cup orange juice
½ cup Ruby Port
½ cup sugar
1 bag fresh cranberries
1 orange

Directions:

Place cranberries, orange juice, port and sugar in a medium saucepan.
Peel three large pieces of skin from the orange and add to the other ingredients.
Cook on medium high heat until it comes to a boil.
Reduce heat to simmer and cook 30 minutes or until cranberries pop, stirring occasionally. Continue simmering until desired consistency.
Remove from heat and remove orange peels.
Place in a container, cover and chill at least 30 minutes.

*Great recipe to make the night before

Cranberry Brie Bites

Ingredients:

1 package pastry dough, thawed
4-6 oz. brie cheese
Cranberry preserves
1 tablespoon butter, melted

Directions:

Preheat oven to 350°F.
Cut pastry dough into 3 inch squares and press into mini muffin pan.
Cut brie into 3/4 inch cubes and put one in each pastry square.
Top each with 1/2 teaspoon of cranberry preserves.
Brush tops of pastry lightly with melted butter.
Bake for 20-25 minutes or until crust is flaky and golden brown.

Cranberry Kale Salad w/ Quinoa

Ingredients:

Salad:
1 bunch of kale
½ cup dried cranberries
1 lemon
½ cup chopped macadamia nuts toasted
1 cup quinoa, cooked
½ cup crumbled goat cheese
Pinch of salt

Dressing:
½ cup olive oil
2 tablespoons apple cider vinegar
½ lemon
Salt and pepper to taste

Directions:

Cook quinoa in rice cooker or in covered saucepan 20-30 minutes. Set aside to cool.
Cut lemon in half and set aside 1/2 for salad dressing.
Wash kale, remove stems and chop roughly. Squeeze juice of 1/2 lemon over kale, add a generous pinch of salt and toss thoroughly with hands.
Toast chopped macadamia nuts in skillet on low heat for 5 minutes or until slightly golden and fragrant.
Whisk together olive oil, vinegar and lemon juice. Add salt and pepper to taste.
Toss all ingredients together with dressing and serve.

Cranberry Wild Rice Soup

Ingredients:

1 1/2 cups cooked wild rice
4 tablespoons unsalted butter
2 carrots, finely chopped
2 celery stalks, finely chopped
1/2 cup onion, finely chopped
4 cups vegetable stock
3 tablespoons all-purpose flour
1 cup fresh (or frozen) cranberries, chopped
1/2 cup dried cranberries
1 cup milk or half-n-half
Salt & pepper to taste

Directions:

Cook wild rice and set aside.
Melt butter over medium heat.
Add carrots, celery and onion.
Cook until tender, about 8 minutes.
Whisk vegetable stock and flour together until smooth; add to mixture.
Add the fresh cranberries & stir until soup thickens, about 5-10 minutes.
Add the cooked rice and dried cranberries.
Cover, reduce heat & simmer, stirring occasionally, until all cranberries are softened, about 15 minutes.
Stir in half and half and continue simmering until warm.
Salt and pepper to taste.

Cranberry Cornbread

Ingredients:

1/2 cup butter (room temperature)
1/2 cup sugar
2 eggs
1 cup milk
1 1/2 cups all-purpose flour
3/4 cup cornmeal
2 teaspoons baking powder
1/2 teaspoon salt
1 cup cranberries (cut in half)

Directions:

Preheat oven to 350°F.
Cream the butter and sugar in a large bowl.
Mix in the eggs one at a time followed by the milk.
Mix the flour, cornmeal, baking powder and salt in another bowl.
Mix the dry ingredients into the wet ingredients.
Mix in the cranberries.
Pour the mixture into a greased 9 inch square baking pan.
Bake 25-30 minutes or until a toothpick inserted into the center comes out clean.
Cool on a wire rack.

Cranberry Pear Walnut Cobbler

Ingredients:

2 cups fresh (or frozen) cranberries
1 pear, peeled and cut into bite-sized pieces
¾ cup chopped walnuts
½ cup plus ¾ cup granulated sugar
2 large eggs
1 ½ sticks unsalted butter, melted
¼ teaspoon vanilla extract
1 cup all-purpose flour
Salt (just a pinch)

Directions:

Preheat oven to 350°F.
Combine cranberries, pears, walnuts and ½ cup of sugar in a 9-in pie pan or 8-inch square baking dish. Toss until coated.
In a medium bowl, whisk together eggs, melted butter and vanilla extract. Add in remaining sugar and mix until blended.
In a separate bowl, mix together flour and salt. Add to wet ingredients and stir until combined.
Pour the batter over the cranberry mixture.
Bake for 40 minutes, until crust is golden and fruit bubbles.
Cool on a wire rack.

Cranberry Citrus Sorbet

Ingredients:

1 1/2 cups water
1 1/2 cups sugar
2 1/2 cups unsweetened cranberry juice
Juice from 1 small orange, lemon or lime

Directions:

In a heavy saucepan over medium-high heat, combine the water and sugar.
Bring to a boil and cook, stirring occasionally, approx. 1 minute or until the sugar dissolves.
Add the cranberry and citrus juices and return to a boil.
Lower heat to medium and cook for about 1 minute.
Remove from heat and cool until it reaches room temperature.
Refrigerate until chilled, from 3 to 8 hours.
Transfer to an ice cream maker and freeze according to the manufacturer's instructions.
Transfer the sorbet to a freezer-safe container and cover.
Freeze until firm. Makes about 1 quart.

ACKNOWLEDGEMENTS

There never seem to be adequate words to thank the many people who help bring a book from initial idea to finished manuscript.

I could not ask for a better editor than Elizabeth Christy, who has the patience of a saint when it comes to working with me on revisions. Her expertise not only makes a manuscript shine, but constantly teaches me about the writing process and about myself as a person.

I'm thankful for the excellent plot suggestions from beta readers Carol Anderson, Jay Garner and Karen Putnam and to Carol for her proofreading abilities. As always, Keri Knutson at Alchemy Book Covers proved she has the magical ability to see through emails right into a person's mind when creating custom artwork. Tim at Book Design and More, and Clare Ayala, deserve kudos for print and eBook formatting services.

Special thanks go to Valerie Peterson, Andi Caruso, Susan Foppiano-Valera and Elisabeth Conley for contributions to Aunt Maggie's Cranberry Cottage Cookbook, as well as to friends and co-workers who were brave enough to taste test items I personally cooked – a frightful task, indeed.

Above all, I'm grateful for the steadfast support of family and friends throughout the development of this book. Their encouragement is what allows random ideas that float around in my head to turn into stories such as Cranberry Bluff.

CPSIA information can be obtained at www.ICGtesting.com
Printed in the USA
LVOW07s0315310815

452162LV00004B/154/P